THE SECRET OF THE MORGUE

THE SECRET OF THE MORGUE

by

FREDERICK G. EBERHARD

RAMBLE HOUSE

ISBN 13: 978-1-60543-759-0

To CHET

WHO SAID THERE MIGHT BE
SOME TRUTH IN THIS TALE.

F. G. E.

The characters in this yarn are purely fictional—
believe it or not.

F. G. E.

Preparation: Jim Weiler and Fender Tucker

Cover Art © 2014 by Gavin L. O'Keefe

CHAPTER I

A MURDER IN SUMMITVILLE

LYMAN K. WILBUR, an able lawyer who had forsaken his profession to become a criminologist of note, sat reading a late mystery thriller in his apartment one afternoon on an early spring day. He threw the book down with disgust.

"They're all alike," said he to himself. "Stereotyped! The plots are hackneyed. In nine out of ten you can guess the guilty party after the first two chapters. They're abominable. They're rotten. All the authors are alike. Rubbish! Twaddle! And someone said big men read them for mind rest. God! Anyone who can stand the rank and file of them doesn't need to worry—his mind's at rest all right. It's dead."

Wilbur walked over to a very smart Volsteadian cellarette and brought forth a decanter from which he poured a rather stout portion. He drank the drink with a wry face.

"The damn liquor's worse than the thrillers nowadays," he continued to himself. "One's at least as rotten as the other."

The telephone rang. He stepped to a small table, picked up the instrument and answered the call.

"Bankers' Indemnity," said he. "Yes. A murder! At Summitville—Cashier of the Citizens Trust? Two hundred thousand gone and no trace of it?—Looks like an inside job? Sure I can go—right away! I'll catch a train at once."

He hung up. "Damn it all," he remarked, as he poured another drink from the decanter and shed his dressing gown. "And I just qualified in the billiard tournament. That's hell!"

An hour later Lyman K. Wilbur was on a train speeding toward the city of Summitville to investigate a murder. At twelve o'clock midnight the next night he arrived in Summitville. He was the only passenger to get off the train. A rather unctuous porter sat his grips on the platform before he alighted.

"Thanks, Mistah Wilbur, thanks," the porter effused, as he pocketed Wilbur's half dollar tip and crawled back on the train.

"How the—" Wilbur started to ask the porter how he knew his name, but the train pulled out.

Wilbur looked around. There was no one about the station. A dim electric light shone above some clicking telegraph keys in the oriel window of the agent's office and lighted the platform slightly. A flickering railroad lantern sitting on the dispatcher's desk seemed to be alive. The train upon which Wilbur had arrived whistled in the distance; a light shot skyward as the stoker fed the engine of the train more coal; and then all was quiet. Wilbur picked up his grip and walked down the platform toward a street. It was the main artery of Summitville. Coming to the street he put his grips down, lit a cigarette and calculated the main thoroughfare.

"So this is Summitville! Ha! I'll bet a damn good drink of Bourbon whiskey the case is a suicide," he said to himself. "This dump would drive anyone to it. A suggestion of murder is outlandish. I'll bet another drink someone's been reading those impossible detective yarns down here. Oh, well, Hell!"

Summitville justified all Wilbur's impressions, if not more. It was located on the junction of a U.S. and a state highway, which roads ran through the place simply because there was no evasion. The place was infected with seven thousand inhabitants. Dog ate dog in the business section. Chain stores alone escaped this form of cannibalism. Customers couldn't park on the main street because all of the merchants had their own cars in front of their own places.

A scab-minded attorney who had a notion that Blackstone was some form of granite juggled the city politics with the aid of underlings who continually and ravenously ate his sop. As a consequence the mayor was an easy shifting sort, the police department a dog pound and the board of works—just that. From the fact that Summitville represented a considerable percentage of the county population, the mange-minded attorney controlled the county officers, and although the county seat was in a neighboring small town it functioned from Summitville. A clique ran everything. There were three large factories in the town, a few small ones and a nursery. Bootlegging flourished. Drinking was the town diversion. There was a chapter of the D.A.R., a women's club, a W.C.T.U.—those necessary organizations for female quid- nuncs and morality righters. A few men with gyratory thoughts made up the Chamber of Commerce. The sunken, the damned, and the moral lepers hung out at Storer's cigar store where they played "rummie," bet on baseball pools or concocted plans for practical jokes. This was Summitville where three rivers met, surrounded by numerous lakes.

Lyman K. Wilbur walked up the main street in search of the hostelry. The street was deserted. The night police were napping after their round of door inspections. He crossed a bridge that spanned the Rat Tail river, went past the statue of a union soldier which stood in the center of the intersection of the two highways, and came finally to the hotel, The Sum- mitville House. An electric light gleamed above the clerk's desk. Wilbur entered the place. Upon the desk under the light was a poorly printed sign which read, "Ring the bell for clerk." Wilbur pushed the bell vigorously.

While awaiting the appearance of the clerk he read a copy of the *Summitville Daily Times*. On the front page was an ac- count of the Morley case, the one in which he was interested. It was as follows:

"After thorough investigation, much thought and delib- eration, the Morley case has been disposed of. The coro- ner's jury came to the conclusion that Eugene Morley was not murdered. It has rendered a verdict of death by sui- cide. We believe the verdict voices a popular opinion. As most readers of the Times know, the body of the missing cashier of the Citizens' Trust was found in his cottage on Ramona Lake. Dr. Simpson and Dr. Clyde, two of our leading dentists, made the identification of the body this

morning. They readily identified dental work which each
of them had done for the late Mr. Morley. The body of the
dead cashier was in a bad state of decomposition when
found. Mrs. Morley definitely identified the body as that
of her husband. Mr. Fellows and Mr. Tully of the Citizens'
Trust also identified it. The dentist's identifications left no
room for doubt. The gun found beside the body was one
belonging to the bank which had been in the cashier's
cage for a number of years.

"Pierre LaVell, our genial undertaker and competent
coroner, said that the clothes removed from the corpse
were those of Morley. There seems nothing to indicate
Morley met foul play as was first suspected. The fact that
there were two bullet wounds in Morley's body does not
indicate a murder, according to Jud Haynes, Lieutenant
detective of police. Detective Haynes says that it is possible for a suicide to shoot himself in the head and then
through the heart, and cites a review of the Burton case in
Newport, R. I., in 1885 by the late Professor Agnew to
prove his point. Professor Agnew demonstrated the fact
theoretically: 1st, a bullet may enter the brain and not
cause the injured person to lose consciousness; 2nd, it
may course the brain and cause no muscular paralysis;
3rd, a man may with his own hand first shoot himself in
the head and a minute afterward shoot himself in the
heart, and 4th, a suicide may first shoot himself through
the heart and immediately afterward shoot himself in the
head. Professor Agnew then cited several actualities in
support of his theory. As we all know Morley was shot
through the head and through the heart. There is only one
feature of the suicide unexplained. No one knows what
became of the defalcator's money, if the money was really
embezzled by Morley."

"That's a hot one," said Wilbur to himself. "The chap that
wrote the article seems to have his doubts that Morley took
the money. Maybe he didn't. And he shot himself in the brain
and through the heart! That's one for the psychopathic ward

even if it has been done. I know it has too. But just because Lindbergh hopped to Paris is no reason to believe that a sparrow can leave Sag Harbor and fly to Deauville. Christ walked on the water too, but nobody else has done it. I'm a little like the reporter on the sheet—maybe Morley didn't embezzle the money."

The night clerk who received almost all of his nocturnal rest the same as any other right living individual in spite of his occupation, appeared as Wilbur made his appraisal of the article.

"Howdy, stranger!" said he as he loped down the stairs in a pair of slapping sandals, wearing a bathrobe and having disheveled hair. "I'm just a little bit late gittin' down after yer ringin'. You'll have to overlook that, stranger."

"I thought something detained you," said Wilbur.

"I'll say there did, brother. But what can I do for you?"

"I'd like a room," replied Wilbur, and with a wink added, "without—"

"Oh, I get you—you slept in one of those city hotels last night. You don't need to worry, mister, we ain't got 'em. If they was one in the house I'd know it too, cause I'm duck soup for the bugs. Sign the register."

Wilbur dipped a spluttering pen in an ink well and wrote his name upon the hotel register which was offered by the clerk. The clerk turned the register and looked at the name.

"Oh, you're Lyman K. Wilbur, eh?" said he.

"That's my name."

"Well sir, they's some folks summerin' out on Ramona Lake asked me to tell you to come out there as soon as you came in."

"But I don't know anyone at this place you speak of."

"Yep. I'll bet you do. This guy's name is Jack Haughton. He and his wife's out there. An' say! His wife ain't hard to look at while yer talkin'. She's got all the females in this town down to bare skin an' fuzz. She don't wear any socks an' ain't got no hair on her legs. An' them pins she's got, mister! The women in Summitville have been tryin' to imitate her and you and me and God knows that a pair of pin-feathered toothpicks can't hold a candle to her'n. You know what I mean. She's built!"

"Yeah!" laughed Wilbur at the description. "That's her I guess."

"Well, Haughton heard you was comin' to these diggin's and he told me to scoot you out to Ramona Lake no matter what hour you came in."

"How do you get out there?"

"Listen, brother, I'll get you out there quicker than it takes to tell. Service is our motto."

"Go to it."

The night clerk reached for the telephone, called a number and soon had a sleepy inhabitant of Summitville on the wire.

"Hello, is this you, Joe?" he asked. "Well, this is Si, up at the Summitville House. I've got a cash customer wants to go out to Haughton's cottage on Ramona Lake." The answer must have been to the clerk's liking for he hung up the telephone with a bang.

"There's a taxi man—this Joe. God, he don't care where he goes at night nor what hour. Keeps his nose clean too. An' he's been in some durn dirty scrapes—boozey neckin' parties that made our paper open up a new sport column. Yep! Joe's all right. He'll be right over. Drives a good car, too—got a heater for winter drivin', and a fan fer summer."

"Thanks!"

"Hm! Don't thank me, stranger. I'll get a little divvy from Joe. An' 'fore I forget about it, this Haughton cottage is right next to the one where they found the dead man. That ought to interest you. Haughton was tellin' me you was quite a detective. Gosh all hemlock, how do you guys look at dead ones all the time?"

"Dead people are harmless, Si."

"Huh!" Si snickered. "They ain't around hereabouts."

"So!" answered Wilbur as he heard the irregular tattoo of a car's motor outside. "I think your friend Joe has arrived."

"Yep, that's him," answered Si. "I know that motor jest like the prayers my ma taught me. He's stalled me between here and Ramona Lake with more women than there is blue gills in the durn lake. An' if you don't think bein' stalled with a married woman five miles from town ain't somepin' to worry about when she's got to be back home on time, you ain't never taken your Ten Commandments seriously."

Si helped Wilbur outside the Summitville House where Joe's car was idling. Si put Wilbur's grip in the back seat and then spoke to Joe. "Take Mr. Wilbur out to Haughton's cottage. He's all right. He's a detective that's here investigating the Morley killin'."

"The papers said it was suicide," said Wilbur.

"Well, I 'spose I hadn't ought to say killin'," replied Si, "but the folks hereabouts for the most part just doubt this suicide business spite what the bladder says. If I've heard one person say Eugene Morley was murdered instead of suicidin', I've heard a hundred."

"What do you think?" asked Wilbur.

"Well, I ain't got much to base anything on, but it's durn funny, I'm thinkin', how Webb Tully, the president of the Citizens' Trust, has come up in the last couple of years. Two years ago he didn't have nothin' much but an outdoor privy, an' now he's got a forty thousand dollar home, drives a swell car, and is finishin' his two kids off east."

"He might have been lucky in the stock market," suggested Wilbur.

"Nope. Webb Tully ain't the gamblin' kind. He's a note shaver, a forecloser, and a penny grabber. He'd take the pennies off a dead man's eyes or the nickels out of a blind man's cup, but he won't gamble. He's got the first dime he ever earned. He ain't the chancin' kind."

"What's your idea of his connection with the Morley case?"

"My idea may be all wrong 'cause I can't back up my suspicions with nothin' but my own ideas, but I'm thinkin' it might'a been pretty easy for Webb to have taken that dough out of the Citizens' Trust an' pointed the finger of suspicion on Morley. You'll find out he ain't givin' out any statement about the bank. He tells everyone, 'The bank examiner found a shortage in Morley's accounts.' That's all. An' I wouldn't put it past him to kill Morley or have someone else do it. He'd do that sooner'n he'd gamble. He's a chiseller."

"Hum!" exclaimed Wilbur as he lit a cigarette and stepped into Joe's car. "That's an idea."

"Yep, an' there's more than me thinkin' that way," replied Si.

Joe put the car of seasonal appointments in gear. "Well, so long boys," waved the night clerk. "An' good luck, Mr. Wilbur. Hope you get the dirty cuss that murdered Morley. Gene was a good kid."

"Good night," answered Wilbur.

Joe pulled away from the hotel and drove down the main artery until he came to the corner where the Civil War was memorialized. There he turned right and followed a paved road which was cluttered with signs advising the tourist and pleasure bent that Ramona Lake lay ahead, signs of the Hotel Fineview and the Cardinal Lodge. Every farm house had a stand in front of it and the price of country eggs and butter flashed in view every few minutes upon blackboards furnished gratuitously to the farmers by the Citizens' Trust. Below the price of the butter and eggs the sign told how far it was to the Citizens' Bank. Signs upon the stands advertised cottage cheese for sale, jellies, frying chickens, fruits, anything that a thrifty country woman could turn into the gold of the realm. Nearer the lake the stands disappeared. The signs persisted but most of them read, "Minnows for sale," or "Fishworms."

"The hotel clerk seems to think Morley was murdered," said Wilbur after they turned at the memorial monument. "What's your idea about it, Joe?"

"I'm thinkin' it was a murder too," replied Joe. "But I think Si is barkin' up the wrong tree. I don't believe Tully did it. In the first place Tully's yellow and ain't got no guts. But there's a bird connected with the Citizens' Trust that might have."

"Who's that?"

"Ambrose Fallows! He's an attorney that runs the works in this county. The runty politicians take orders from him.

He's the 'big shot.' Every damn officer in this county is under his thumb an' on account of his power in the county. I guess his bark is heard upstate too. And he's a director in the Citizens' Trust."

Wilbur whistled.

"Seems to me his ratin' in Dunn and Bradstreet's been risin' fast the last two years, too," Joe went on. "He ain't done it flashy like, with a fine home and a big car. He's too damn smart for that. He just keeps on goin' around like a hayseed. He's gone right on livin' in an ordinary frame house an' drives an old Model T Lizzie. But they do say as how he's invested plenty away from home. It's my opinion he's gettin' plenty out of county graft or else he got into the Citizens' Trust. It wouldn't surprise me none that he had Morley bumped off to cover his tracks. I can't believe Gene Morley would do anybody for a thin dime, much less bump himself off. There's skullduggery somewhere."

"This Ambrose Fallows would do such a thing, you think?"

"Hell yes! He'd kill Christ if there was a quarter in it. An' what makes me more suspicious of him than ever is the fact that he went out of town the night Morley disappeared. I know, 'cause I took him to Central City. But keep that under your hat 'cause I ain't said nothin' about it before. An' he didn't return for a couple of days. I don't know where he was an' don't think anybody else does."

"Well," Wilbur thought to himself as the taxi driver recounted his theory, "I guess the big towns don't furnish all the smart ones. And I think I'll have to change my first impression of Summitville. This case looks like it might be complicated."

"It's a rotten business," the driver continued. "I don't think there's anything to it but murder. That state detective says a man can shoot himself through the head and then shoot himself through the heart but damned if I believe Morley did."

"It's about four weeks since Morley disappeared?"

"Just about three weeks."

"And the body was found day before yesterday?"

"Yes, sir."

"Well, a lot can happen in a week and more in three weeks."

"Yes, sir, you said something, mister. The insurance company was pretty decent to Mrs. Morley, I'm thinkin'.''

"Oh, Morley had insurance?"

"I'll say he did! Fifty thousand dollars. Just as soon as the suicide verdict was given out they plunked over the dough, too. That Integrity Mutual is all right. They're sort o' proud of settlin' claims promptly."

"Mrs. Morley was the beneficiary?"

"Yep, she got it all."

"Another one for the book," said Wilbur to himself.

"That was a tough break for the insurance outfit," Joe went on. "Morley'd just had the policies for five years."

"Long enough to get by the suicide clause."

"Yep, that's what I heard 'em say. Well, it all just goes to show I've always been right. I always says that just as soon as a man begins gamblin' on his life his luck's goin' to chance. I'm superstitious-like. Take me for example. If I was insured for fifty thousand dollars I'd be worth more dead than alive by a damned sight. An' let me tell you somethin', mister! If I was insured for fifty thousand and my wife knew it I'd be coffin fodder before next Labor Day."

"You don't mean that Mrs. Morley—?"

"Oh no! I'm not insinuatin' Mrs. Morley had a thing to do with this job. I don't know, of course, but I'm thinking she ain't that kind of a woman. But my woman! Say! She'd cackle at my last gurgle if it meant fifty thousand smackers to her."

"Well, Mrs. Morley is just another idea," said Wilbur. "It's been done, you know, in some of the best of families. A man's a man for a' that, and a pot of gold is a pot of gold. A woman can get a man most anytime but money is a little elusive. I have known of instances where women made marrying quite a profitable business."

"I wish you wouldn't bring that up. It gets me jumpy. My wife was married to two men before she got me. Both of them died an' she got a little insurance out of both of them. The fact is, I bought this car with the insurance money her second husband brung her. You got me thinking."

"But you haven't any insurance, or so I inferred."

"How in hell do I know with all these big newspapers givin' accident insurance policies with subscriptions? She may have me lined up swell. I could be croaked accidentally and she'd draw one of them double indemnity things. Nobody would be wise. I'd just be number three and she would be lookin' for number four. I'm going to find out about this thing."

"Don't get excited, Joe. There's nothing to worry about. I'm sorry I brought the subject up."

"The hell there ain't nothin' to worry about! We're takin' *The Chicago Graphic*, *The Detroit Fast Press*, and *The Cleveland Square Dealer*."

"Oh, that's nothing," answered Wilbur as he suppressed a laugh. "She probably loves to read."

"Yeah! An' what she's probably dyin' to read is a notice of my passin'. Come to think about it, I've had two accidents with this car lately. I found my revolver cocked in my inside pocket the other morning and my last batch of home brew exploded the other night just as I was reachin' for a bottle opener. You don't suppose she's got anything planted on this road? You know some of them paper policies pay more if you're killed while ridin'."

"No, Joe, I think your fears are all groundless. Those little experiences you have had are what I call happenstances. You've just got jumpy, as you put it, over this Morley affair."

"Well, maybe so," Joe answered. "Nevertheless I'm goin' to be careful from now on an' I'm goin' to find out about those papers we're takin'. Fact is, we ain't got no business takin' more than the *Summitville Times*. That's a durn good paper, too—furnishes a lot of readin'."

Joe whirled the car around a bend in the road and Ramona Lake loomed up ahead. A full moon was setting on the western side and its beams sparkled upon the lake water which was gently waving. Cottages lined the shores and at this late hour there were lights in many of them. A sail boat tilted in the wind—some youngsters for whom a day's sailing was insufficient. There were numerous small boats—lovers, no doubt, canoes, and one mad racing speed boat. What a night! Not one for a murder.

"It ain't goin' to be long now," said Joe, as he guided his machine into the rough and sandy road which skirted the lake shore and led past all the cottages. "Your friend's cottage is up this road about a quarter of a mile. And right next to it is the Morley cottage."

"That's what Si told me."

A few moments later Joe pulled up in front of a smart looking cottage within which lights still gleamed.

"This be it," said Joe as he applied the brakes in no uncertain manner. "An' the folks are still up. That's luck."

The front door of the cottage opened and Jack Haughton peered out. "Is that you, Lyman?" he yelled.

"Yes," replied Wilbur. Thereupon Jack burst from the door of the cottage and ran down the inclining boardwalk to where Wilbur stood. His wife took his place in the doorway. Jack seized Wilbur's hand and shook it warmly. "Well, you old son of a gun!" exclaimed Jack heartily. "It's sure good to see you. Who'd have ever thought you and I would get together in this neck of the woods? Come on in. Where's your baggage?"

Joe passed the baggage out and Wilbur paid him for the trip in a generous way.

"Thanks! Much obliged!" said Joe enthusiastically as he noted the size of the bill. "You can get me anytime at the Summitville House—that is, providin' the old lady ain't aimin' on spendin' the accident insurance."

"Good night, Joe," replied Wilbur. Joe turned around and his tail light hopped along down the winding lake road. Wilbur and Jack climbed the slight rise which confronted the cottage, with Jack carrying the baggage. Mrs. Haughton flashed the porch light on and all three met under its glare.

"Alice!" cried Wilbur as he grasped her outstretched hand. "You look wonderful. One would never know you were the same person that rescued your estimable husband and myself from the hands of that demon in the Rockies. You look marvelous."

"Oh, you old flatterer!" replied Alice, as she kissed Wilbur and added, "Jack doesn't mind. I really don't know what you would do if you didn't have some woman to cajole. Come right in, though, I'll forgive you again." They entered the cottage.

"Well, how on earth do you happen to be here and how did you learn of my arrival?" asked Wilbur after they had seated themselves inside the cottage. "That's a mystery to me."

"You tell him, Alice," said Jack. "I'm going to prepare three highballs to celebrate this occasion." Turning to Wilbur he added, "You're not on the wagon?"

"Not yet. I doubt if I ever shall be again. I've vowed that I could lie to myself no longer. But I hardly expected to bow before the shrine of Bacchus in these parts. I was under the impression that I was now in an arid desert."

"Oh no, my dear Wilbur. This area was well represented in the repeal column of the Digest Poll. This is what is popularly known as a drunken dry area. The gentle art of circumventing the prohibition law is at its best in this community. It's really enlightening, this countryside. It broadens one. They are very urban in their tippling. You find most everything here that one does in Bellevue in New York— everything from *Jake paralysis* to *mania a potu.*"

"Very illuminating to me, I must say. The great American joke!" laughed Wilbur as Jack went to the kitchen. "Now about my question," said he to Alice.

"It's rather a simple tale," replied Alice. "Since our marriage Jack and I have been honeymooning here and there. About six weeks ago we passed through here and the lake intrigued us. It's really a delightful spot in the daytime.

"I fell for the beauty of the place at once and so did Jack. The fishing is excellent. To make a long story short we bought the place and expect to keep it for summer vacations. We moved in here just a week before the man was murdered next door, having remained at the Summitville House during the time that the cottage was being redecorated. The tragedy hardly interested us at first, being used to murder melange as we were."

"I can readily understand," answered Wilbur. "After that affair at Folsom Lodge. A gruesome thing that. But go on."

"When it became known that the murdered man had such a shortage in his accounts and that the Bankers' Indemnity had to make this good, Jack became interested, inasmuch as he is one of the directors in the United Bankers' Indemnity. He became suspicious of the affair when there was no trace of the missing money. Of course he wired the Indemnity company and requested that you be detailed upon the case. Besides the fact that it promised to be of some interest, we also thought you might enjoy a vacation with us. That's how you happen to be here and why we knew you were going to arrive."

"Very nice! I am sure I am going to enjoy the visit with you folks but I am not at all enthusiastic about this murder case. From what I have been able to glean out of the Summitville paper, the hotel night clerk and the taxi driver who brought me out here, I believe it's just a question of elimination until I lay my hands on the guilty party."

"Perhaps you may be fooled. This countryside looks entirely inoffensive and the natives anything but blasé, but such is not the case, as we have found out in our short sojourn here."

Jack returned with a tray upon which were three sparkling highballs. "These are very good despite the fact that we are far from our favorite bootlegger," said he as he held the tray forth so that Alice could select her glass. "The whiskey is more than uncommon in quality—from the western province of Canada, British Columbia." He proffered the tray to Wilbur, who picked up a glass, and Jack continued, "I hope international bootlegging continues in spite of the drastic attempts to curb it until such time as our moonshiners develop a very palatable and safe brand. The natives around here who do their guzzling with the homemade product tell me that improvement is noted in every run."

"That's encouraging," Wilbur remarked, as he sipped of the highball and commented, "It has a very excellent aroma, and an exquisite taste."

"I thought you'd like it," Jack replied. "Were you surprised when you found out we were here?"

"Surprised! That isn't the word. I was dumbfounded—bowled clear over. I might have imagined however that you had something to do with my visit here. I'd forgotten that you were interested in the Bankers' Indemnity. What is the lowdown on this affair?"

"That's what I want you to find out. It would appear to me that a gala band of crooks are flourishing in this little out of the way place. This case won't be as exciting as the Milliken affair, I'm sure, and let us hope it isn't, but nevertheless I think it is going to present some unique features. I suppose you are acquainted with the salient facts?"

"No, I know very little about this case—just what I gleaned from glancing over the Summitville paper and what the night clerk of the hotel and the taxi driver told me. I take it you know most of the story."

"Your knowledge then must be meager. The inhabitants about here have voiced every possible theory, I assume, except the right one. You know a country community does nothing but talk about one of these affairs continually. As a result stories are contorted and actually changed. However there are certain things which are verified facts. The newspaper has contained nothing but what certain people probably intended they should publish. If it's not too late I'll run over the affair with you. Alice and I are a couple of night owls, you know."

"Go ahead," replied Wilbur. "I'm not at all sleepy or fatigued. Your effort at dispensing spiritus frumenti has caused me a temporary insomnia at least."

"Eugene Morley disappeared the night of May second," Jack began. "But first I'll take you back and give you a little

of his history. There is little known about his early life except
for the fact that he was born in the New England states of
ordinary parentage and that he struggled through his adoles-
cent years much in the fashion of many young men, blacking
boots, peddling newspapers and washing spittoons. He
learned, as it were, from a meager schooling, the streets and
toil. At an early age he gravitated westward and fate led him
to the diminutive city of Summitville. There he entered the
Citizens' Trust for the first time as a janitor, one of the many
odd and lowly jobs by which he made a livelihood. He engaged the attention of Webb Tully, the president of the bank,
and from then on his rise was spectacular. He became the
cashier, married one of Summitville's most estimable young
ladies and was regarded as a model citizen. He was supposed
to be a respectable home-loving man. It is not known that he
had a ticker-tape complex. He was more than frugal with the
opposite sex. Toward the church he was plethoric. In short he
had none of those qualities which often cause the sudden
disappearance of widows' mites and children's pennies. I'll
digress a few moments and give you some idea of Webb
Tully.

"Webb Tully is a man who has his fingers in every pie.
His main source of money, however, is the Summitville Casket Co."

"What a familiar chord!" exclaimed Wilbur. "I always run
into casket manufacturers, mummy collectors, or some form
of burial parasite."

"It seems that the casket business was at a low ebb a couple of years ago," Haughton went on. "Whether the people
weren't passing out with due regard for the undertaker and
his henchmen, the granite and flower salesmen, I don't know,
but be that as it may, the Summitville Casket Company was
on its uppers. But in the last two years the Casket company
has been going like nobody's business. It has been rumored
that Webb Tully may have appropriated from the bank to pre-
vent a bankruptcy action against him. At the same time his
manner of living has been on the upgrade. He lives very ex-
travagantly. His home is an elegant affair, his car an ultra-

modern one and his family enjoys everything, denying themselves nothing."

"I learned a part of what you have just told from the night clerk."

"No doubt. He's a loquacious sort. Well, to get back to Morley. On the night of his disappearance he was about town in many places. He visited Tully at his home, was seen in conversation with Ambrose Fallows, quite a city politician, and of whom I'll say more later, was at home a part of the evening and was seen last upon the street as late as eleven o'clock. After that he was never seen until his body was discovered in his cottage which is next door to mine.

"Now for the peculiar features of the case. On several occasions following Morley's disappearance the cottage next door was subjected to inspection. It was an easy matter to look in the windows into each room. It was possible to learn in this manner whether any person, or person's body, was within the cottage.

No person, or person's body, was seen at any of these inspections. Then day before yesterday Mrs. Morley and Pierre LaVell, a Summitville mortician, the county coroner and close crony of Morley, came out here to clean up the cottage for summer tenancy. They discovered the decomposed body of Morley lying on the bed in one of the rooms. Now we come to the strange occurrence which prompted me to send a wire to the Bankers' Indemnity. The undertaker and Mrs. Morley had no keys with which to open the cottage. They expected to break in. But when they arrived, lo and behold one of the windows was open. All of them at other inspections of the cottage had been closed. And now listen closely. LaVell would not allow Mrs. Morley to look at the corpse at this time. He took her to Summitville, then came back alone, took the clothing from the corpse and burned it—everything but a suit of underwear. Yesterday morning some boys who were wading in the lake in front of the cottage found Morley's key ring in the water and upon it the one key to the cottage. Now I ask you, Wilbur, do you think that a man contemplating suicide would throw the key to his locked cottage into the lake and then enter it a hard way—by opening a window which was nailed down on the inside?"

"What? What's that?"

"Exactly what I said. Every window was nailed, I examined them. They were nailed, in fact, so no one could raise them from the outside unless they broke the windows. Do you think a suicide would enter his cottage by way of the door, lock the door, raise a window, go down to the lake, throw the key away, come back to the cottage, enter it through the open window and then take his life?"

"No! A suicide wouldn't do it. He wouldn't be that painstaking. Of course I can see where he might if he had a reason to make his death appear as a murder for a purpose—say a large insurance where the time of non-payment of the policy for suicide was not up. Those clauses usually hold for two years."

"That's exactly what I thought when I wired for you."

"Hum! Damn!" exploded Wilbur. "The case does sound interesting. I fear it's not as simple as I anticipated. What about this attorney, Ambrose Fallows?"

"Well, that's another part of the riddle," Haughton went on. "He's a director in the bank. He controls the city politics of Summitville and for that reason also controls the county. There is reason to believe he has a considerable fortune but you can't lay your finger upon it. He looks like a moron but he's far from it. His manner of living is that of a man hard pressed. But to the point! He overbears all the constituted authorities. In his hands they are as so much clay. He could make the coroner do his bidding. He exercises the same power over the sheriff and prosecutor."

"In a murder case the French say *Cherchez la femme.* Is there any woman?"

"Well, there's Morley's widow. She came to the cottage with LaVell. About three months ago he secured a divorce from his wife. He's been trying to sell his undertaking business."

"Ever been any talk about LaVell and Mrs. Morley?"

"Not a rumble until now."

"There's a possibility, that's all. If LaVell did the murder, fifty thousand dollars and the loot from the bank would make a neat little sum for a couple to embark upon the sea of matrimony. I was told Mrs. Morley was paid that right after the coroner's inquest. Be that as it may, she and LaVell are suspects. Any other woman who might be mixed up in the case?"

"Nothing except a rumor."

"Sometimes rumors are worthwhile."

"Well, this one is a sort of intangible thing. You'll understand when I tell you. It seems there was some woman summered on the lake last year who went by the name of Mrs. Browne. No one knew where she came from or anything else about her. She came suddenly, remained a couple of months, and departed as suddenly as she came. Very few people made her acquaintance. It was rumored that Morley was seen in her company. Understand, there was nothing positive about it. There's no one to be found who will vouch for it. He might only have met the woman casually. You know the wrong construction is put on things like that many a time. For instance, someone might have seen you kiss Alice tonight. I might have already gone into the house. A vicious story might have been spread."

"Not much to that story, I fear. Well, we've four suspects—Webb Tully, Ambrose Fallows, Mrs. Morley and Pierre LaVell. Any one of them might have committed the murder."

"Yes, and there might be a collusion. All four may be implicated. I don't go in for the suicide business at all."

"Me either. The coroner and others have probably destroyed anything which an inspection of the cottage would reveal?"

"They probably have. Everything was gone over so there's but a slight chance that any evidence remains. I don't believe one could find a finger print or anything else of value. In fact the cottage was thoroughly cleaned from top to bottom."

"That's a shame. But nevertheless we'll have a look at it in the morning. Something may have been overlooked."

"I wish you would. Your eyes see more in a minute than the whole state department of safety would see in a week."

"The jury, Jack," Mrs. Haughton prompted her husband. She had remained very silent up to this point. "Tell Mr. Wilbur of that while I fix some more highballs." She collected the empty glasses.

"Oh yes, that's a peculiar thing," said Jack. "The coroner's jury returned a verdict without ever seeing the body. It was empanelled and undoubtedly hand picked by Fallows or LaVell. I talked with Ed Fox, one of them, relied upon to be non-talkative but nevertheless loquacious, and he told me that they were taken before the casket of Morley to render their decision. At the time he remarked to the coroner, 'We don't know whether there is a body in the casket or not,' LaVell replied, 'You'll just have to take my word for that.' "

"Hum! That's a strange thing. There must have been some tell-tale clue of the murder within the casket. Someone was probably fearful that some inquisitive juror might ask too many questions concerning the two bullet wounds."

"It's a strange affair. With such suspects and a political machine to toss monkey wrenches, I'm afraid the case is going to be a tough one."

Alice returned with the highballs. Wilbur drank his with satisfaction.

"There's another mystery," said he as he held his glass up. "Rattlin' good whiskey for a place like this—better by a damn sight than the stuff you get in New York where the ways are greased and easy."

"It's not at all hard to get, either—quantities—pints, quarts, cases or otherwise."

"I'm certainly getting interested in the community," laughed Wilbur. "It's a revelation to me. I've heard of the wide spread distribution of alcoholic products but thought the thing was exaggerated. Hum! Damn it, I don't believe the half has been told. And at first sight I thought this hole was the deadest spot it had ever been my misfortune to connect with. The liquor is a life saver, anyhow. But why shouldn't bootlegging flourish in a community where they can get away with murder? It steps up a murderer's courage and then after the deed it mellows his remorse. But getting back to the Morley case, what about the gun? Any finger prints on it?"

"I understand there were. Plenty of them! An expert from the state department of safety took them. They didn't prove anything, however."

"Why not?"

"The body was decomposed and they couldn't get any of the corpse."

"Hum! That's right. It must have been badly decomposed if no prints could be recorded."

"It was. The fingers were rotted away to the bone. And rats had been at the body. No impression was possible."

"The four suspects! What about their impressions? Were they taken?"

"I can't say positively. I don't think so. I think a monkey wrench was thrown into the investigation at that point and if there were any inquisitive people who wanted the thing done they were told to mind their own business. It was just one of those things."

"I don't imagine any of the four will object to finger printing?" Wilbur chuckled.

"They may."

"They can. It's a constitutional privilege but it's done right along in spite of the privilege. Police officers do it almost universally. I'll ask each one of them to submit to the printing but if they object I won't force the issue. Damned if I don't hate to use police methods. Browbeating never gets them anywhere. If any one of them objects that will be a lead in itself—a pointer. There'll be a way of obtaining information to convict afterward. There'll be nothing circumstantial about the evidence either. And that's another thing I'm against. One thing more: has the body been buried?"

"Not yet. The funeral is set for tomorrow."

"It may not occur tomorrow," was Wilbur's laconic reply as he looked at his wrist watch. "That's enough for tonight, or rather this morning. We'll get up early and inspect the cottage. Let's visit a while—forget murders and suicides. Then we'll tumble in. I know Alice is tired of gruesome chatter."

"Oh no, not so long as you two boys are enjoying yourselves. In fact I'm getting so I love the morbid side of life. I've been that way ever since I almost witnessed a slaughter of the two of you."

"Is that nice?" asked Wilbur. "One might imagine you were sorry you saved us from being murdered—and I don't know but what it might have been a good thing."

"How is your snake collection?" asked Jack.

"Oh, I've added a few since I last saw you," Wilbur grinned. "I'm still a collector while you are not. Your collection of feminine rejections stopped with Alice's acceptance of you, I believe. What is your hobby now?"

"Trying to stump one of the cleverest criminologists in the world today."

The conversation turned to those things which are common to close friends, reminiscences, and topics of the day. Finally after a last salvo from the bottle they retired.

CHAPTER II

THE MURDER COTTAGE BURNS

EITHER FROM THE UNCOMMON RESULT of more than passably good liquor or because of the tension occasioned by the mystery, Wilbur slept fitfully. His bedroom was on the north side of the cottage and the window to his room faced the Morley cottage which was some two hundred yards away. Outside it was one mass of darkness, for the moon had disappeared. Long before it had gone down the lake revelers had come to shore. There was a forbidding stillness without, broken only by the lake water as it lapped the shore. In one of his moments of wakefulness while peering out of the window into the blackness of the night, the criminologist thought he saw a light. If he did it was a flash, for by the time he sat bolt upright in the bed and rubbed his eyes it was gone. He strained his ear but there was no sound to be heard except the noise made by the water at the shore. There was no immediate repetition of the light. After some moments of staring into the blackness, Wilbur sank back upon his pillow content in the thought that the flash had either been a visual aberration or a mental thing. He dozed. How long he dozed he had no means of knowing but the next thing he remembered was being awakened by a loud knocking at the cottage door. He looked out of the window and before his eyes was a lurid scene. The blackness had been dissipated. The air, the night, seemed to be aflame.

Jack had arisen and was going to the door.

"Who's there?" he cried as he groped at a wall button which turned on the living-room lights.

"Harmeson!" replied a voice from the outside. "I live in the cottage just south of you. The Morley cottage is on fire."

Before Jack succeeded in turning on the lights in the living-room, Wilbur knew the cause of the light outside. He would have known it in an instant had he not thought that his vision had played a trick upon him before when he thought he had seen a flash of light. The entire cottage was in flame, consumed almost in one fiery burst, or so it seemed.

"Someone set fire to it," said Harmeson when Jack finally opened the door and looked out into the light. "It's been soaked in oil. You can smell it. There's no use in trying to put the fire out. The cottage is gone up. But I thought I'd arouse you. A few flying sparks might set your place off."

"Well, thanks, old man for arousing me," replied Jack. "I'll dress and see that he won't burn up too."

As Harmeson left, Wilbur entered the living-room, closely followed by Alice.

"It's the Morley cottage," Jack explained to Alice who hadn't as yet comprehended what had happened. "It's burning up." Turning to Wilbur, Jack added, "We'd better dress and watch this place."

"O.K."

Both men dressed as quickly as possible and made their way to the Morley place. When they arrived there, a number of the cottagers stood about conversing. The flames were subsiding, the sparks were no longer shooting skyward and what had once been a cottage was being rapidly reduced to a smoldering mass. The odor of kerosene was distinct. The heat was too great for any close inspection at this time.

"Incendiary, all right," said Wilbur.

"No doubt of it," returned Haughton.

"Who did it and why? There was some tell-tale evidence in that cottage. That fire just about disproves the suicide theory completely. I wish I could have had a look inside of that place. There was something. Oh, well, whatever it was it's gone now. Damn it!"

"Why wasn't this done when the body was there? It would have destroyed all of the evidence, including the body."

"That thought came to me. Had Morley been burned up, though, the insurance would not have been paid because there would have been no proof of Morley's death. This looks very much to me like positive proof that the widow is entangled in the murder. It strongly points toward Mrs. Morley and LaVell. It is my impression that Morley was murdered some place away from the cottage and his body placed in the cottage after death. There was a reason why the body had to be discovered. It was either on account of the insurance or because the murderer wanted to stop the hunt that was going on. That hunt might have proved disastrous to some people we have mentioned. The finding of the body and the suicide verdict put an end to the search for Morley and the verdict ostensibly clears the murderer. But the master reason is this—burning of the body would have clearly established the case as a murder. A man doesn't suicide and then burn his body up, especially after inflicting wounds through his head and heart. No, Jack, there are very good reasons why this fire did not happen when the body was in the cottage and I am afraid there are some very good reasons why the fire happened after the body was removed."

"There must have been some evidence which could not be removed from the place."

"It appears so. There must have been something damaging to the suicide theory, not removable except by destruction. What was it? At the present I haven't the slightest idea. Maybe we'll be able to find out later, but I'm afraid not. First we want to keep everyone away from the place until I can inspect the ground about it. The ground is damp and we may find footprints which will identify the party that fired the cottage. After that a close inspection of the ruins will be in order. Perhaps the evidence they sought to destroy did not burn. I don't believe any of the cottagers have been close yet."

"Hell no! Most of them have been scared to go near it. The countryside has conjured up all sorts of weird stories about the place since the body was found. I've heard every sort of tale. It's been haunted. Mysterious lights have been seen inside of it at all hours of the night, to hear the natives talk."

"Well, I saw one either in it or right outside of it sometime before it was fired," said Wilbur. "There was one there to-night. I slept spasmodically and during a wakeful spell I saw it."

A peculiar noise broke on the night air from the lake. Wilbur and Haughton turned and listened. It was the hum of a motor. It didn't sound like the hum of a motor boat engine. It was more like the motor of an airplane. And then as both men listened and looked, two lights flashed on the water of the lake far down the shore on the right. The hum increased in volume and the lights began to move toward the center of the lake, gathering momentum as they went. There was a roar. The lights lifted from the water. Higher and higher they lifted. The roar faded into a slight drone. At last the lights faded from view.

"An aquaplane," said Wilbur. "That looks mighty queer."

"Whoever set fire to the cottage escaped in that plane," answered Jack.

"No doubt of it. There's mystery! What does that mean, an aquaplane taking off at this hour in the morning under a cloak of darkness? And where did it come from?"

"Hum! I never heard it come in."

"No, neither do I imagine anyone else did. It probably settled in with a cutoff motor just before the moon disappeared. They'll cruise around until dawn and then land somewhere. Well, that's something to investigate. There's not such a large number of such ships on the Great Lakes. It ought to be easy to locate. As soon as day breaks we'll investigate the point where it took off."

The heat from the burning cottage was abating and an approach to the burning ruins was possible even though it was uncomfortable. The curious cottagers had left. Cautiously scanning every bit of ground with a flashlight, Wilbur searched for any clue which might lead to the perpetrator of the arson. There was no success in this painstaking effort until he reached the spot where the back door of the cottage used to be. Here there were distinct footprints. They were undoubtedly fresh.

"There are the prints," said Wilbur to Haughton who was close beside him.

"I see them," answered Jack. "But they only increase my bewilderment. Those prints are—"

"Yes, they are the footprints of a woman beyond any doubt. They go in and come out."

"But—"

"Don't try to figure it out. Take your car and go directly to the Morley residence in Summitville. Ascertain if Mrs. Morley is in the city. I'll continue my investigation of the cottage."

Jack proceeded to do as Wilbur directed. Wilbur continued to go over the ground again and again.

After thoroughly satisfying himself that he could find nothing more than the footprints, he returned to the Haughton cottage.

"What'll you have, Mr. Wilbur?" asked Alice who had arisen and dressed. "Whiskey or coffee?"

"Never mind making me any coffee. I'll take about three fingers of straight whiskey and get back to work. I just ran over to get some of my paraphernalia. We found some very interesting footprints and I'm anxious to make a permanent record of them. I sent Jack into town on an errand."

"Here's your whiskey," said Alice, as she brought forth a full bottle which she had just opened. "Help yourself."

Wilbur took a generous helping of the whiskey and then busied himself in his baggage. In a few moments he left the cottage carrying numerous things in his arms. He returned to the spot where the fresh prints were and went to work. He poured a quantity of incandescent charcoal into a special receptacle, lit it and then placed a warming pan over it. Next he heated earth to 220 degrees Fahrenheit and with stearic acid made a cast for a mold. It was the method of M. Hougolin to make permanent records of footprints. Wilbur had finished making the molds and had thoroughly examined them when Haughton returned.

"What's the dope?" asked Wilbur.

"There's no one at home," replied Haughton. "I met LaV-ell going out on a case and he said she left for some town up north and would be back tomorrow. He said she left on the train you came in on—the midnight."

"Oh he did, eh!" exclaimed Wilbur. "The hell she did. That's lie number one at least. No one got on the train at Summitville. Are you sure LaVell was going on a case?"

"Well, he said so and had his ambulance out."

"Maybe so then. But an ambulance would make an excellent get-away car. I never thought of it before."

"Mrs. Morley wasn't home, that's certain. Did you find anything else besides the prints?"

"Nothing except them," replied Wilbur as he pointed to the four foot impressions. "There are two impressions of a right foot and two impressions of a left foot. Do you notice anything peculiar about them?"

Wilbur focused one of the flashlights by whose glare he had worked upon the prints.

"I see the prints, that is all. Yes, there's something funny about them, but I don't know just what it is. They're Friday's footprints for all I know."

Wilbur picked up the molds. "I made these permanent molds after the method of M. Hougolin," said Wilbur as he held them in the rays of the flashlight. "If you will notice, each right one has the heel worn off in a peculiar manner. Each left one shows no such condition of the heel but shows the sole of the shoe is worn off on the left side rather strangely. Whoever our lady of the shoe may be, she wears off her right heel and her left sole just like the molds show."

"Well, then, when we find a woman who does that, it ought to be easy to establish the identity of the party who fired the cottage, providing her shoes are the size of those imprints."

"Hush! Hush! Not so fast, my dear Jack," replied the criminologist. "That is a popular idea. But the facts are, the foot and its print in soft earth or other soft substance do not accurately correspond, one being larger or smaller than the other."

"It doesn't seem possible."

"Nevertheless that is the case. The observation has been checked and counter-checked in Europe by the Surete and Scotland Yard. What we have discovered is just a bit of evidence. It will only serve to corroborate other evidence should we obtain any more. Let's take these molds to your cottage and await the dawn. Leave the tripod and pan. They're too hot to handle."

In Haughton's cottage a few moments later Wilbur displayed the results of his genius and pointed out the peculiar features of the shoes which made the prints. Alice listened attentively and then turned to Wilbur.

"That's clever," said she. "Very clever! But I did not burn the Morley cottage."

"Who said you did? Those footprints are not yours."

"I think I've heard you say you did not believe in coincidences?"

"And I certainly do not."

"Ho! Ho! Here's one time you'll have to believe in one. I wear my own shoes off in exactly the same manner—the right heel and the left sole. If you don't believe me I'll show you."

"Show me."

Thereupon Alice removed her shoes and handed them to her guest. Wilbur surveyed them quietly a few minutes and matched them with the molds. His face flushed.

"Hum! Hell! That's one on me," said he in a study. "Those molds and your shoe heels and soles are alike as two peas. It's got me. There's a sweet case of circumstantial evidence! You are sure no one has broken into your cottage and stolen a pair of your shoes?"

"I don't think so," replied Alice, with a mischievous twinkle in her eyes. "But I'll see."

She left the room to inspect her stock of footwear.

"What do you make of that, Jack?" asked Wilbur. "People have been convicted of crimes upon such evidence. If you'll recall I just told you a while ago that those prints were only corroborative evidence. Now they're not even that, for we know damn well Alice was in the house and couldn't have fired the cottage. And yet she could have made the footprints."

"It must be a coincidence," replied Jack.

"Yes, damn it, it must be but I've never believed in them. It simply takes the wind right out of my sails. That's been one of my greatest assets in all of my cases. And now I pretty near have to admit there is such a thing."

Alice returned. "My collection of shoes is O.K." said she, as she held forth two more pair. "Here's two worn pair of the same kind. My good ones are not worn. That habit of mine has kept one shoe manufacturer, I really believe."

Wilbur inspected the two pair of shoes and admitted defeat. "Well, it's a coincidence," said he. "It's just got to be. There is such an animal. That's tough for me to swallow. Those prints were fresh, but—You haven't been about the Morley cottage lately, Alice?"

"I have never been near it, not at any time," replied she.

"Hum! Damn!" exclaimed Wilbur. "Let's have a drink."

"That's an ideal solution," joked Jack as he started to arise.

"Allow me," said Alice. "I'm used to starting fires."

The drinks were once more produced and once more consumed. Such is Volsteadian swiftness.

"Has any aquaplane ever landed on the lake since you took up residence here?" asked Wilbur after the stimulant.

"I never saw one before," answered Jack. "One could have landed a number of times, though, and I not know it. Airplanes pass over so frequently one pays no particular attention to them. There's an air mail route over the lake and several passenger lines go over it also."

Wilbur looked at his watch. "Let's get going down the lake. It's about daybreak," said he. "We may find out where that plane took off. There's a chance they forgot something in their haste. Have you any idea where it was?"

"It seemed to me they took off at a place called Baker's Landing. If it wasn't there it was close by." Turning to Alice Jack added, "You'd better go back to bed and get some sleep. You look as if you needed it."

"I'm going," Alice nodded. "Cinderella is on her way."

Wilbur and Haughton left the cottage. Dawn was breaking. The fog was lifting along the edges of the lake and fish were flopping. A flock of coots rocked idly near shore. From nearby barnyards cocks crew lustily. It was an exhilarating morning.

Wilbur and Haughton walked lazily along toward Baker's Landing. They arrived there just as the sun burst luridly in the east.

"The plane took off somewhere in this neighborhood," said Jack. "This is Baker's Landing. It's about the best spot on the lake to land. A plane could taxi near to shore."

"Then keep your eyes peeled," admonished Wilbur as he himself began to scan the sand. "Look out for the imprints of a woman's foot."

"You notice the sand, don't you?"

"Yeah, funny lookin' stuff."

"That's Ramona Lake sand. There's nothing like it any place else."

"Peculiar color."

"No one's ever found a cause for it. It's that way all around the lake."

"Hum!" grunted Wilbur as his eyes roamed about over the peculiarly colored sand.

"Oh, oh!" exclaimed Jack. "Here they are." He pointed to the unmistakable tracks of a woman's shoe in the soft lake sand.

"Right!" exclaimed Wilbur as he knelt and examined the tracks. "Same heel and the same sole." He followed the tracks to the edge of the lake while Jack followed the prints the other way until he lost them.

"Hey! Come here," yelled Wilbur when he arrived at the water's edge. Jack went to him.

"Look at those other prints—a man's. He wore boots."

"Someone carried the woman out into the water to the plane."

"Sure! No doubt of it," answered Wilbur as he scanned the water's surface. There was nothing floating anywhere.

"What's that?" asked Jack, pointing on the ground. Wilbur looked in the direction of Jack's pointing finger. Lying upon the sand was a woman's glove.

"A woman's glove!" exclaimed the criminologist. "There were no finger prints left in the cottage. You can be sure of that."

Wilbur picked up the glove and fingered it. "It's a Kayser silk glove," he continued. "Hum! Here's something funny."

"What's that?" asked Jack.

"The little finger is stuffed. The woman has lost her little finger on the right hand. She's made a little cushion to fit the little finger of the glove. Another clue! She certainly took no chances of leaving telltale evidence behind her—using gloves and then the fire."

"Let's see that glove," said Jack who had an amazed expression upon his face.

Wilbur handed Haughton the glove. Haughton looked it over and removed the cushion which fitted accurately in the little finger of the glove.

"Damnit, that's just as strange as the shoes, Wilbur," said Haughton, and he looked curiously at Wilbur. "My wife wears a right hand glove like that. I'm positive, too, that she has never been near Baker's Landing."

"Your wife!"

"Yes. Her little finger on the right hand has been missing ever since a child. It was cut off in a lawn-mower."

"I never noticed it."

"You wouldn't, even with those hawk-eyes of yours. She is very sensitive about it and manages to keep it out of sight. I don't believe I've ever noticed it myself more than a couple of times. She wears Kayser gloves."

"Well, that's coincidence number two. More circumstantial evidence! It's certain there's another woman besides your wife who wears off her shoes in the same manner that she does. She evidently wears the same kind of peculiar right handed glove, that is, providing your wife hasn't been in this neighborhood and dropped hers here inadvertently."

Haughton wore a worried look. "I don't think she has ever been down here. I'm worried, Wilbur."

"Well, don't worry, old fellow. Worry never did anyone any good," replied Wilbur with a slap on Jack's back. "The glove seems to be all there is of interest here except the presence of the prints. We'd best be going back to the ruins of the cottage and look that over before some of the early lake risers come along."

"O.K."

They trudged back to the smoldering mass that was once the Morley cottage. As yet there was no one snooping around it. It was light enough now to make a detailed examination. The structure above the ground was completely destroyed. All that remained was the basement. In it were smoldering pieces of woodwork; a mass of charred material which had once been siding, joints and uprights. As Wilbur surveyed it his keen eyes noted that there had been a singular bit of construction in regard to the flooring. It appeared that there had been a double floor.

"That excites my imagination," said he as he called Jack's attention to his observation. "Why should a lake cottage be built with a double floor? Why a double floor like that in any place? If you will notice, Haughton, those two floors have been at least three feet apart, making a room, a closet, a hiding place or what have you. The construction was ingenious. When the building was standing I don't believe anyone would be able to detect the fact of the double flooring, despite the fact that there was a cellar. But why two floors?"

"It might have been a soundproofing device, so that no one in the house could hear anything that was going on in the cellar."

"Well, what might have been going on in the cellar?"

"Counterfeiting! Gambling! A murder! What might be going on in anybody's basement in these days of prohibition? It might have been the 'Winegar woiks.' "

"Quite so! The murder of Morley might have taken place there."

"I said murder."

"I said Morley's murder might have taken place there. But I don't think so. I don't take much to your soundproofing theory. I believe the space was created for some special purpose—a cache perhaps. The ground slopes gradually away from the level of the top flooring on all sides. The outside entrance to the cellar is some distance from the cellar wall and the ground is about three feet lower at that place. Coming into the cellar by that entrance one would think he was under the one and only floor to the cottage. Entering the cottage one would have no suspicion of a second floor. I'll venture a guess that before this cottage burned down there was a trap entrance to the upper floor and a trap exit to the lower."

"What could the space contain that it would be necessary to hide?"

"Oh, any number of things," replied Wilbur with a shrug. "We'll probably never find out."

At this juncture Wilbur picked up a long pole which lay upon the ground and began poking about in the cellar debris, moving half consumed particles of timber to peer anxiously into the recesses he created by so doing. Jack watched his maneuvers the while, keeping his eyes open for anything unusual that might be revealed. At one corner a section of both floors had caved into the cellar and had been only partially consumed by the flames. Wilbur shoved a mass of rubbish from the edge of this flooring and a ghastly sight was revealed. Protruding from the edge of the flooring were two human feet.

"Another mystery! Another murder!" said Wilbur to Haughton as he exposed the gruesome sight. "There's the reason for the burning of the building."

"Who can it be?"

"I haven't the slightest idea. But whoever it is, it's a woman."

"A woman?"

"Sure, those feet are those of a woman."

"What'll we do."

"Get that body out and look it over before anyone else does. But how are we going to get it out? We can't raise that flooring without a great deal of time-consuming work. Anyhow it is too hot to get down in there yet."

"I've an idea."

"Spring it. You've always got the ideas."

"I've a strong piece of rope in my cottage. We can loop one end, slip the loop over the feet, tighten it up and pull the body out."

"Bully! That's good. Get the rope."

Haughton ran to his cottage, secured the rope and returned. They looped the rope and Wilbur lowered the loop to the protruding feet. Haughton guided the loop over the feet with the aid of the pole which Wilbur had been using. A pull on the rope tightened the loop. Then both men pulled on a line as much parallel to the body as was possible. Luckily the body was not pinioned between the two floors. It moved with the first pull. Slowly, more easily than they anticipated, the body issued from its hiding place between the two floors.

"Let's pull her entirely out," suggested Wilbur. "We'll say we thought she might have some signs of life about her if the coroner says anything about it." Together they pulled again. Up came the body. Up, up it came. Finally they dragged it over the top of the cellar wall. It lay on the damp ground, a terrible looking spectacle. The body was burned badly. The clothing had been consumed by the flames and the form was entirely nude.

"Go get something to throw over her," said Wilbur. Haughton dashed to his cottage and brought back a blanket which he spread over the corpse.

"Terrible! Terrible!" said Wilbur. "The hair is all burned off and the face is charred almost as bad as some of those timbers. Does she resemble anyone you know? I mean of course her stature and general appearance. No one could recognize the face."

"It's no one that I know."

"Maybe your wife might know her. Women usually scrutinize other women closely."

"I'll call her. The sight of the body won't affect Alice." Haughton left to call his wife. While he was gone Wilbur took out a pad and pencil which he always carried for just such an emergency. He knelt down by the corpse and noted everything he saw—jewelry, probable height and weight; probable age; the presence of any visible birthmark, wen, scar, mole, vaccination mark, blood or injury. He typed the head as to shape and form; made a note of a high forehead and prominent eyes, the latter's color. The ears which had almost escaped the effects of the flame he noted as having been pierced. The neck he described as short and thin with a large mole on the right side. Her form was jotted down as being an almost perfect thirty-six. He recorded her hands as being beautiful, the fingers long and tapering with well kept nails. He finished with some other general observations just as Haughton returned with Mrs. Haughton.

Mrs. Haughton looked at the still form upon the ground and shuddered. "Yes, I believe I know her," said she. "I think it is Mrs. Morley."

"Mrs. Morley?" said Wilbur, incredulous.

"I can't say positively but I believe it is."

CHAPTER III

WHOSE FOOTPRINTS?

JACK WENT TO THE HARMESON COTTAGE and called LaVell, the coroner. Wilbur covered up the head of the corpse.

"You may as well go back to the cottage, Alice," said Wilbur. "I'll remain until the coroner comes. Jack will be back in a few moments."

"What is it, Lyman—a suicide or a murder?"

"It looks like a murder to me but somehow or other I've a hunch that it's going to be called a suicide. If the coroner has his way I think it will be a suicide. Right after I discovered the footprints I sent Jack to Summitville to find out whether Mrs. Morley was at home. She was not. Your husband met LaVell out at that hour with his ambulance. He told Jack that he was going on a case. Jack asked him if he had seen Mrs. Morley. He replied that Mrs. Morley had left town that evening on the train upon which I arrived. No one got on that train at Summitville."

"Oh, I see! You think—"

"I surmise. LaVell was probably the last one in Summitville to see Mrs. Morley. An ambulance could move a dead body and not create any suspicion. On account of the death of Morley himself it could be backed right up to the Morley house and the body of Mrs. Morley removed without its presence exciting any suspicion if it were seen there. LaVell could bring it out to the cottage, deposit the body and then set fire to the cottage. That hypothesis leaves the footprints unexplained. And there are no tracks of LaVell evident. But there's the cellar way. It opens up on the grass where no footprints would be seen. Perhaps Mrs. Morley was not brought here dead either. She could have been very much alive and in the ambulance. It might have been a tryst. She could have entered through the back door, arranged for an entrance through the cellar, have returned to LaVell and both of them entered through the cellar way. As a last explanation the footprints need not necessarily be Mrs. Morley's."

"Yes, I comprehend. There are numerous ways the affair could be accomplished. You'll agree that these little out of the way places do have their mysteries though."

"And how!"

"Well, I'll run along back to the cottage. I see Jack coming. I'll be getting you boys some breakfast."

Jack came trudging up in a few moments and a little while afterward LaVell arrived, accompanied by numerous residents of Summitville. Authoritatively he began his inquest. A score or more of people identified Mrs. Morley from her general appearance. An engraved wedding ring on her left hand made the identification complete. As in her husband's case a dentist identified her plates as having been made by himself. They were comparatively recent and bore a mark by which he identified his own work.

Harmeson was questioned, as were Wilbur and Haughton, in the presence of a jury hastily assembled. A verdict of accidental death was rendered. After the verdict the undertaker LaVell placed the body of Mrs. Morley in a dead basket and removed it to his morgue. The morbidly curious milled about the ruins of the cottage. Wilbur and Haughton went to the latter's cottage. While Alice went ahead with her preparation of breakfast, the two men discussed the case further after the usual highball.

"It was just as well that they delivered that verdict and removed the body," said Wilbur. "As soon as the excitement dies and the sightseers leave I want to examine that basement further. I don't believe Mrs. Morley burned up in that cottage accidentally, although she might have. She could have come out there for the express purpose of burning the place up, saturated the rooms above, crawled into the space between the floors, saturated that, and then burned when the fire started accidentally before she was ready for it, but I don't believe it. Personally I think something happened to her before the fire. I think someone intended to cremate her."

"Well, this happening proves one thing to my satisfaction," said Jack as he sipped at his highball. "It shows how incompetent officials are in criminal cases. And between you and me, it's a perfectly asinine system that permits a layman to be a coroner. God! If I was in the murdering business I wouldn't want any sweeter territory than a place where a layman was the coroner. They're incapable. The medical examiner system is the correct one. But try and tell this Anti-Saloon Leagued country anything outside of hair-trigger enforcement of the great American vassalage. Right now that death is explained to the complete satisfaction of the nincompoops by that slip-shod half-baked coroner. They're satisfied. But if they suspected that quart was sitting on the table there they'd have every officer in the country trying to find it and they'd keep on the job long after the contents was in headaches and purple parrots."

"And did you see how they all looked at us when we told them an airplane took off from the lake?"

"Yeah!" laughed Jack. "They've heard about flying boats but don't believe one can fly. They thought we were kidding. They think the wheels would sink the fuselage. If you'd mention the word amphibian to them they'd think you were talking about a sea serpent. The way they looked us over I guess they thought we'd just lammed from the booby hatch."

"And who was that hawk-faced fellow that kept snooping around the edge of the cellar all the time?"

"Oh, that was Ambrose Fallows. The fellow with him was Webb Tully."

"Aha!" exclaimed Wilbur. "Our little banker friends! I thought they were very much interested in the remains of the cottage. Mrs. Morley's death didn't seem to interest them much."

"Maybe the cottage hadn't burned to suit them."

"Something about that cottage cellar engrossed them, that's sure. Well, so far we've two corpses, the imprints of some lady's shoes and a lady's glove. Oh, by the way did you tell Alice about the peculiar glove?"

"Not yet."

"Alice!" said Wilbur. "Did you ever see this glove before?" Wilbur took the glove which he had picked up at Baker's Landing from his pocket and handed it to her. She examined it.

"Why, of course," she replied. "That's one of mine."

"One of yours?" said Jack.

"Why, certainly, dear," she replied. "Where'd you find it?"

"Down by Baker's Landing," Jack answered. "Right where the plane took off. When were you down there?"

"Why, I was never down there in my life!" she exclaimed in open-eyed astonishment.

"Are you sure that's your glove?" asked Wilbur. "Take a look at your effects."

Alice left the room to inspect her supply of gloves.

"You didn't see where her finger was missing when she examined the glove, did you?" Jack asked Wilbur.

"I surely didn't."

"Well, you never will in the ordinary course of events. That's a regular sleight of hand trick with her."

Alice returned carrying her gloves. The little finger of the right handed ones were padded in exactly the same manner as the glove found on the lake shore.

"I was mistaken," said she as she held out her gloves. "I have all of mine."

Wilbur examined and compared the gloves. "Hum! Damn! Another coincidence! I'm losing my cunning or else I've been playing hunches all along. It looks as if Lady Luck had faced about too. Someone else has a right hand with the little finger missing. The most peculiar thing about it, though, is the fact that you and the other woman use the same identical kind of cushion to fill out the finger. Those cushions are all made of the same kind of silk."

"Hum! That is perplexing," grunted Jack.

"Well, talk it over at the table, boys," said Alice. "Breakfast is ready." They sat down to breakfast.

"The glove affair and the shoe affair make me feel like a rank amateur," Wilbur remarked as he took a piece of toast. "If this thing keeps on as it has I'll be playing with building blocks, cutting out paper dolls and riding in a kiddy kar. My clues are just like sailors' sweethearts. There's one in every port and they're all equally false. I think you were wrong when you said you thought I'd enjoy my vacation."

"Oh, but you're hardly started," said Alice as she poured the coffee. "You only came last night. I think you've done remarkably well."

"Yes, I feel like a very celebrated criminologist," returned Wilbur with a laugh. "I'm good. Another murder has been committed right under my very nose. That's what I call rubbing it in. I wish I'd have crawled out of bed and gone over to that cottage when I saw the first flash of light. I might have saved that woman."

"You might have," replied Jack as he squirted some grapefruit juice into his eye. "And then again that might have been the last time you'd have seen any light. And really, old dear, I don't believe you'd make a good cinder even though you are partially saturated with alcohol. Besides, it seems to me that these murderers hereabouts make really abominable looking corpses out of their victims. The Chicago method is much better, don't you think?—where they give you a sieve-like expression?"

"Oh, Jack, behave yourself. We're eating breakfast," admonished Alice.

"So we are," replied Jack. "Excuse me, honey."

"Let's leave our further inspection of the cottage ruins until later," suggested Wilbur. "Didn't you say they intended to bury Morley today?"

"That was the intention of the widow," replied Haughton. "But the way things have turned out I wouldn't be surprised that Morley's burial is off for today. It will probably be postponed in order that there may be a double funeral."

"You'd better go down to Harmeson's after breakfast and telephone LaVell. He'll tell you if there's any change in the plans. You needn't tell him who you are. If there's a change in the plans we'll go ahead with our inspection of the Morley place and if there isn't we'll go right in to Summitville. I want to get a peep at Mr. Morley before somebody gets six bucks for shoveling the dirt out of where he's going. You know what I mean."

"You mean before he has to be dug up."

"Righto! Excuse me, Alice. I also forgot we were breakfasting."

"Oh, that's all right. Don't mind me. I've eaten with you two crime-mongers so often I expect graveyard soup and pickled heart at each meal."

"Oh ho! And I guess that will hold you, Mr. Wilbur," roared Jack. "I'll run down to Harmeson's and do the telephoning at once."

Upon calling LaVell Jack learned that the funeral of Eugene Morley had been postponed. He had been right in his supposition. There was to be a double funeral. An uncle of Mrs. Morley, the nearest relative, had made the arrangements.

"Good!" said Wilbur when Jack returned and informed him of the change in the burial plans. He arose from the breakfast table. "Now let's get to work. I'll get into some old clothes if you have any about. I think we can roam around in that cellar now. It may not be comfortably cool yet, but the sooner we get busy the better."

Jack procured an old suit of clothes. Wilbur donned them. Jack also changed into old clothes, and together they returned to the ruins of the cottage. The stone walls were still hot but once in the cellar they found the heat not unbearable. Equipped with a long crowbar Wilbur began to explore the debris systematically, turning over everything in sight. It was work, hard work, and consumed almost the entire forenoon. He watched carefully for clues as he did so.

Haughton took his turn at the crowbar when Wilbur tired. If system would unearth anything of importance they had it.

Around the edge of the cellar above them a crowd of specta-
tors looked down. At the point where the body of Mrs. Morley had lain, about six feet of the flooring remained uncon-
sumed. It had fallen into the cellar, preserving the aperture
between floors at the one end and narrowing at the other to
an approximation of the two floors. It was in the V-shaped
aperture so produced that the body had lain.

"That's puzzling," said Wilbur, as he rested from his labor.
"Did Mrs. Morley crawl into that floor compartment and accidentally burn up? If so, why was she trying to burn up the
cottage? Or was she killed and her body placed there by
other hands? If she was killed why was she killed? What was
the reason for the double floor? So far our search has revealed nothing to solve any of these questions. Get an axe,
Jack, and we'll knock out this upper flooring."

Jack procured an axe and together they battered out what
remained of the upper flooring. This effort revealed nothing
further about the death of Mrs. Morley but it did bring something to light that was interesting. Between the flooring
along the far wall reposed several cases of liquor. Printed on
the cases was the brand, "Coon Hollow."

"There's the secret of the two floors!" exclaimed Wilbur
as he broke a case open. "It's been a cache for liquor."

"Pass it around," yelled some bystander who stood above
them.

"Morley's private stock, perhaps," said Haughton.

"I don't think so," responded Wilbur. "The compartment
has been too large. Furthermore why should he keep it out
here instead of in town at his residence if it was his private
stock? The cottage has been unoccupied since last summer
and a man would hardly leave such a large quantity out here
to be taken by vandals. To tell you the truth, Haughton, this
is not wholly unexpected by me for I have noticed much
glass all through the debris. From the amount of glass I have
noted I would imagine this secret hiding place was about half
filled with those cases when the cottage burned."

"You think Morley may have been involved in the illegal
liquor traffic?"

"I suspect as much."

"That might be. It would furnish a motive for the murder of Morley and his wife."

"I'll say! A perfectly good motive! He might have been tramping on someone's toes. He might not have split properly with someone he was in league with. And he might have been feared as 'a squawker.' If he was in the business there's any God's number of reasons why he might have been knocked off. When one gets into the great American business he soon finds out that it is highly competitive. A traitor in the liquor business is worse off than a spy in war. Let's dig around further. There's more that we must learn. Who was in this illegal business with Morley? There were others, that's sure. He worked in the bank and applied himself there closely. Someone else must have had charge of this business a part of the time. Do you suppose it might be Fallows, or Tully, or both? Remember they were very much interested in these ruins."

Wilbur had spoken directly into Haughton's ear in a subdued tone so that the curious onlookers above them might not hear.

"Something's rotten," replied Jack. "I've a hunch there's an exit out of this cellar besides the ones plainly evident. I'm going to sound out the walls."

"That's a clever idea. Go ahead. I'll keep stirring this mess up while you do."

Haughton began a methodical examination of the cellar walls and Wilbur continued to pick about in the dying embers. Jack had progressed about half way around the cellar when he suddenly called to Wilbur.

"Come here!" said he. "I've found an exit." Wilbur approached him and Jack pointed to a spot in the wall. "Every one of those cement blocks comes out," Jack explained to Wilbur's amazement as he pointed to three tiers of blocks. "That's no plaster in between them. It's putty." He took his penknife and demonstrated the fact of the putty.

"Clever camouflage! Damn clever!" said Wilbur. "Let's take the blocks out and see what we find."

They removed the cement blocks which comprised the three tiers presumably cemented together. The blocks were still uncomfortably hot so the work was a bit tedious. After a time, though, they removed all of them and a doorway stood revealed which led into a recess of blackness.

"Go get two of my guns, Jack," said Wilbur when the opening stood disclosed. "And bring a flashlight or two."

When Jack returned with the flashlights and guns both men entered the door and disappeared. They found themselves within a corridor which was perhaps four feet wide with no visible end. Where it led to they had no idea, but with guns alert they went forward. Wilbur led the way, flashing his light upon the floor and walls. They took their time and advanced cautiously. On and on the underground channel went.

"Stay close to the left wall," said Wilbur. "You'll notice footprints in the middle. They may prove of importance. Follow right behind me."

"O.K."

"It took a long time and a lot of work to put this over," Wilbur whispered as they went forward. "It wasn't tunneled out to satisfy a whim either. This thing was fashioned for a purpose. One might imagine this in a novel but to actually find it in the neighborhood of Summitville is almost beyond my comprehension."

"It almost proves Morley was engaged in some illicit traffic, either liquor or narcotics, maybe both. An underground affair like this can have but one meaning and that is certainly a sinister one," replied Jack.

"It's a long thing. It doesn't seem to have any end. This was a job, if you ask me. Judging from the surface of the walls and the underfooting it's been used some time. Whatever the racket it's been going on for years."

On and on they walked. Finally the end of the corridor appeared ahead. Both men ceased talking and stealthily approached. A door barred further progress. It was locked.

"What'll we do?" asked Jack.

"Step back a little," ordered Wilbur. "I'll shoot the lock out." He leveled his gun at the lock and pulled the trigger. The sound of the shot reverberated down the underground passage. The door opened up without further difficulty. But another obstacle loomed. They stood facing a wall of concrete building blocks. It was another wall the like of which was in the Morley cottage. They removed the blocks easily and stepped into the boat house at Baker's Landing.

"Another proof of the connection between the flight of the aquaplane and the Morley murder," said Jack as he looked around him.

"Undoubtedly," replied Wilbur, as he likewise cast his eyes about the room. "But what's it all about?" He strolled about the boathouse and examined the entire interior in his meticulous way. His eyes scanned the floor.

"It's been scuffed from dragging something about, probably boxes," said he as he pointed to marks on the floor. "They've been dragged from the doorway." And then his eagle eye fell upon something lying upon the floor. He stooped and picked it up. It was a shank button covered with a blue serge material. He inspected it closely and passed it to Haughton.

"Hold on to that," said he. "Put it away safely in your pocket."

"It's only a button," observed Haughton.

"I know that very well. But a man might burn on account of it. It's not an ordinary button. It's not a button with perforations. It's a shank button. Furthermore, it's covered with serge material. Whoever that button belongs to wears a blue serge suit. Do you see why it may be valuable?"

"Yes, some one of the people we suspect may be wearing a blue serge suit which is minus a button."

"That may be so and again it may not. We'll see. Who owns the boathouse?"

"I don't know."

"Well, that's something we'll have to find out." The boat house was combed for other evidences of occupation but no success attended the effort.

"Well, that's that," said Wilbur who possessed the uncanny faculty of knowing when he had exhausted his resources. "Let's go back through the tunnel. There's no use going outside. We were all around this place this morning. While going back we'll give the tunnel another once-over. I don't know why but I've a peculiar suspicion that those footprints we avoided coming down tell a story. Keep to the right." They entered the tunnel and Wilbur began to examine the footprints that were plainly visible in the center of the tunnel floor.

"You are not anticipating any more lady slippers?" asked Haughton.

"No," returned Wilbur. "The ground is too damp. But we might run across a cowslip. I'm fairly certain in my own mind that something slipped. Notice carefully. There are two footprints. One set, the larger footprints, are coming down the tunnel from the direction of the cottage, and note—the man who made them came down twice. The other, the small footprints, are going toward the cottage. The person who made them went in that direction once and did not return."

"Yes, I see that plainly."

"I wish now I had taken the man's footprints at the beach. Anyhow I think I know enough. The large prints were made by a boot and unless I am greatly mistaken the same boot made the prints on the shore."

"The aviator?"

"Either the pilot or someone who was with him. That's important but I fancy I see in these large and small prints something that is more important. The door at the boathouse end of this passage was locked on the outside."

"What's strange about that?"

"My dear Haughton, there's nothing strange about it. The man going out locked the door on the outside, that's all. A man going toward the cottage couldn't lock it. The man making the small footprints never returned but the man making the big prints did."

"It's too deep for me, Wilbur."

"No, it's not, Jack. Use your eyes. Notice the imprints. The man supposedly going out imprints his heel a great deal more than the man coming in, whereas the man coming in imprints his sole more than the man supposedly coming out. But that only holds for one set of the big prints."

"I'm stumped."

"No, you're not. Reason it out. They were both going in the same direction and were in this tunnel together. They were carrying something heavy."

"Oh, I get you. The man making the big footprints was walking backward when he made one set of his tracks."

"Correct. He came back alone, and locked the door on the outside. And what might these two men have been carrying?"

"A corpse! Sure as hell."

"Right again. Whose corpse?"

"Mrs. Morley's."

"No! No!" Wilbur said, almost in disgust.

"Why not?" asked Jack.

"Mrs. Morley had no button on her dress like that shank button. You can wager on that. And I don't believe you'll find any of the suspects wearing a blue serge suit that is minus a shank button."

"What's your idea?"

"Continuing my reconstruction of what happened, I think two men carried Morley's dead body through this tunnel from the boat house to the cottage. His coat was buttoned tight when his body was brought into the boat house. The two men laid it down for some reason—rest or something. When they went to pick the body up again the blue serge covered button was torn off."

"Hum! Damn it, that's clever reasoning. I only hope you don't find that any of my shoes fit those big tracks. If mine do and the little ones run off on the heel of one and the sole of the other Alice and I are stuck."

"Quit kidding. I'm reconstructing what actually happened. It sounds plausible, doesn't it?"

"More than plausible. I'll bet that's what actually happened."

They finished the rest of the underground passage and came to the cottage end. They emerged. The group of curious onlookers was still present.

"Do any of you know who owns the boat house at Baker's Landing?" asked Jack.

"Sure—to—to—tootin'," stammered Buck Peters, a lake character. "It be—be—longed to Mr. Mo—Mor—Morley."

"That settles that," said Wilbur. "Let's go to your cottage, indulge freely just once and get busy again. I scent something big in this case."

CHAPTER IV

A SHANK BUTTON

"THE MORBID THRONG had a good party while you were gone," was the greeting of Alice when they entered the cottage.

"How's that?" asked Jack.

"Someone of them climbed into the crematory and secured the cases of whiskey. They passed the bottles around and had a rousing good time. The sheriff happened along, confiscated what was left and the song was ended for a time. Those who imbibed went down the lake road and from what I heard the melody lingers on."

"Oh, the sheriff just happened along?" said Wilbur. "Likely! I wouldn't be surprised that Ambrose Fallows sent him out with explicit directions to get the liquor."

"Wonder why he didn't bother to see what we were doing in the tunnel?" pondered Jack.

"He knew all about it, most likely," replied Wilbur. "And figured we might as well have our fun. But I must say he is a charitable cuss to take the liquor. I'll bet he sews his baby up for the winter if he's got one, and tells his prisoners there's no Santa Claus. A big hearted boy, he is."

"Don't crab, Lyman," put in Jack. "The officers must have rewards."

"What did you learn, boys?" asked Alice. "I'm curious. I walked over to the cottage, saw the mysterious tunnel and everything. Did you see any pirates, meet Al Capone or rescue a blonde?"

"Wilbur's got track of something," laughed Jack. "There's a big track and a little one. He thinks the big one is that of a dinosaur and the little one that of an invert. I differ with him. I insist that the big one was made by Robinson Crusoe and the little one by Friday."

"But honestly, I'm interested," said Alice. "I think this is simply a gorgeous mystery. I always imagined such things existed only in the minds of mystery story writers."

"Well, if you must know, the tunnel ends in a boat house," answered Wilbur.

"Oh, that's not at all exciting."

"Oh, it might be," answered Jack, who had started to wash. "Supposing it housed ferry boats."

"My gawd, you don't mean to say they have boats," Wilbur spoke up. Jack laughed heartily. "Listen, you eggs! What's it all about?"

"Morley was in some kind of a racket—liquor, narcotics, or maybe both," Wilbur replied seriously. "The cottage was a cache, the tunnel a means to take the contraband to the boathouse and the boathouse a place to load out unobserved. From footprints in the tunnel it appears that two people carried something, we'll say it was a body, from the boathouse to the cottage. In the boathouse I found a coat button. That's the sum and substance of the knowledge we possess from a rather exhaustive examination of the cottage cellar, the tunnel and the boathouse."

"Oh, I'm disappointed. That's not at all exciting."

"It's not a great deal to be proud of," Wilbur admitted. "But I feel certain that it is a beginning. The button, I believe, is important." Turning to Jack, Wilbur said, "Show her the button."

"It looks just like an ordinary button to me," Alice commented, after she had examined the button. "It might belong to anyone."

"That's just the point. I don't believe it is an ordinary button," Wilbur explained. "We'll see later about that. Didn't the coroner burn Morley's clothes when he found the body? Did you tell me that or did I read it in the paper?"

"I told you," answered Jack as he wiped his face on a towel. "The coroner burned them up."

"I wonder where he burned them. I hope he didn't do it in the cottage."

"I don't imagine he did," Alice put in. "Most all that's ever in one of these cottages is a gas or kerosene stove. I suspect he did it outside. There's a pile of ashes, a sort of refuse heap, behind the cottage."

"Good! That sounds promising. I'm excited. Let's examine the ash pile. You know wool clothing doesn't burn readily and lots of times burning pieces are easily smothered. Let's see what we can see."

Wilbur, Haughton and his wife went to the rear of where the Morley cottage had stood and Alice pointed out an ash pile of some proportions. Together Wilbur and Haughton sifted the pile. They almost despaired of securing any reward for their efforts when suddenly the last pile of unsifted ashes revealed something startling. Two shank buttons lay on their improvised screen when the ashes had gone through. The cloth covering of one had burned completely, but around the edges of the other was a narrow rim of blue serge.

"Ain't that sumpin'?" said Wilbur in ecstasy as he fondled the two buttons in his hands. "It proves that a number of my conjectures are right. Morley wore a blue serge suit the coat of which had blue serge covered shank buttons on it. The matching of these buttons supports my contention that the button in the boat house was torn from the coat when the body of Morley was lifted by the two men who carried it. The three buttons almost prove that Morley was murdered. Now, why should LaVell want to burn the clothing? What was there about it incriminating? Why the murder? What was the motive?"

"It might be one of a number of motives. There are those which we have spoken of before. One of them is definitely out, however—the insurance. Mrs. Morley's death removes her as a suspect and his life insurance as a motive. In its place, however, there is Morley's evident connection with illicit traffic. That could furnish a number of motives in itself. And another suspect looms in place of Mrs. Morley: the next of kin. The uncle will inherit the entire Morley fortune.

The uncle may have committed both murders. I'm presupposing Mrs. Morley was murdered, of course."

"There are many motives for Morley's murder," Wilbur replied. "They're all plausible. It's difficult to single one out which is more plausible than the other. Which one is most likely to connect Morley's murder with that of his wife? I surely think she was murdered. Why was she killed? Did she know too much? If she did what did her knowledge concern? Was it bootlegging, absconding, or something else? There's a number of unanswered questions. All I have definitely in mind at the present are the three shank buttons from the coat of Eugene Morley. I feel that this vicinity has given up about all the information it can. Let's go back to the cottage, dress and drive to Summitville."

At Haughton's cottage Wilbur and Jack shaved. They changed clothes and were soon on their way to the city of Summitville, that quiet unobtrusive place where Wilbur at first thought there could not possibly be any crime. The run was made in quick order with Jack's high powered car. He parked it in front of the Citizens' Trust and they alighted.

"We'll stay away from Ambrose Fallows and old man Tully for the moment at least," said Wilbur as they stood and decided their plans. "We've nothing on them at present and might get ourselves into trouble. All we have is hearsay gossip which links them with this thing. That's all. Right now I think I want to interview the tailors. Those shank buttons are in my mind and they keep poking at my intellect. After the tailors I'm sure that I want to see LaVell."

Wilbur looked up and down the main thoroughfare of Summitville, his eyes searching for a tailor's sign. Finally he spotted one. "There's a tailor," he said. "Felix Simon, the sign reads. The name sounds as if he might be rather fat and jovial, bench-legged and likable. Let's give him a call."

"You're doing the detecting."

"That has the earmarks of a nasty remark," said Wilbur as they started for Felix Simon's establishment.

After climbing a flight of rickety stairs Wilbur and Haughton reached a landing from whence a maze of hallways led to lake real estate offices, dentists' torture chambers, beauty shops, insurance agents' hangouts and other offices one might expect the denizens of a small city to inhabit. After coursing these various hallways they came to a door which led into Mr. Simon's shop. They entered.

Felix Simon, after the manner of his kind, sat cross-legged upon his bench. He was mending a pair of breeches which had been badly torn in a road house brawl.

"Hello, gentlemen," said he. "What can I do for you? A nice suit? Beautiful patterns in the book. I'll make you a nice suit."

"How's business, Felix?" asked Wilbur.

"Rotten, thanks! Al Hoover still does the presidenting, the noble experiment has become nobler and the drouth—oh hell! Gott und Himmel, what's the use? Business! There must be a hell—business has gone somewhere."

"I'm Mr. Wilbur, an investigator," said Lyman, with a laugh. "If business is so bad I'll probably not annoy you. And I really hate to annoy people when they are busy. I'd like to ask you a few questions which concern the death of Eugene Morley if I may."

"Me? How should I know anything?" asked Felix in bewilderment.

"The questions are not concerned about the actual murder. I wondered if you ever fashioned any clothes for the late Mr. Morley?"

"For Mr. Morley!" exclaimed Felix. "Did I? I should say so and then some. I made all of Mr. Morley's clothes. His death is a terrible loss to me. He was one of my best customers. Sure I made his clothes. They had to be tailor made. He was one of those few that remain who can't be fit by Hard, Shatterem and Farce."

"Fine," answered Wilbur. "You're just the man I'm looking for. Did you make a blue serge suit of clothes for Mr. Morley the coat buttons of which had shanks instead of eyes?"

"Coat buttons with shanks? Me?" answered Felix in a tone of disgust. "Never! Always I use the buttons with the holes in them. Mr. Morley never wore blue suits. For some reason or other he detested the color of blue. Many and many are the times I have tried to sell him a blue suit. He always wore a black or brown."

"Might he have had a suit made elsewhere?"

"Mr. Morley? No, sir! I have made his clothes ever since he came to Summitville. He was one of those customers that stick with a man. Ach Gott! If it isn't bad business it is death that's robbin' me."

"Well, thanks, Mr. Simon. Your information is very much appreciated," replied Wilbur. "I'm sorry we disturbed you."

"Never mind! I sew by the deaf and dumb system. Talking and hearing don't disturb me. Look at the patch." Felix picked up the pants and displayed the result of his needle-work. The conversation had not affected it.

"Now for LaVell's," Haughton said laconically.

CHAPTER V

THE UNDERTAKER

PIERRE LaVELL was what Wilbur described as "lousy." He never looked another man in the eyes. His demeanor showed him to be evasive, sly and cunning. "He'd cut his own mother's throat for a nickel," said Wilbur. "In the criminal world he'd be a 'rat.' " Further description of him would be superfluous. He greeted Wilbur and Haughton with no great enthusiasm as they entered his funeral home.

"As you no doubt have been informed, I am Lyman K. Wilbur, an investigator for the Bankers' Indemnity," said Wilbur by way of his introduction. "And this is Mr. Haughton, a personal friend of mine."

"Glad to know both of you," replied LaVell but his expression belied his words. "I have met both of you before, at the Morley cottage, I believe."

"At the ruins of the cottage," Wilbur graciously corrected.

"Quite right."

"I am investigating the death of Mr. Morley, as you have no doubt surmised. I understand you are the undertaker in charge of Mr. Morley's body, and also the county coroner," Wilbur went on. "Could I have a few words with you concerning the case?"

"Most assuredly. Why not? Step inside." LaVell was trying to take the interview lightly. At his invitation Haughton and Wilbur entered the funeral home. LaVell showed them seats. He himself sat down after considerable purposeless movement. He was nervous despite an attempt to control himself.

"Now, Mr. LaVell, I have been told that Mrs. Morley and yourself found the body of Eugene Morley in the latter's cottage. Is that correct?" said Wilbur.

"Quite correct," answered LaVell.

"What was the occasion of this discovery?"

"The disappearance of her husband had unnerved Mrs. Morley. She thought a residence at the cottage might help her to get hold of herself. The cottage had been unoccupied for a considerable length of time and of course Mrs. Morley wanted to clean it up before she occupied it. But on account of her husband's disappearance she was afraid to go there alone. Since I had been a close friend of the family, she asked me to accompany her, which I did."

"What was she afraid of?"

"I take it she was afraid of finding her husband's body there, as we unfortunately did."

"The cottage, you say, had been unoccupied?"

"Yes."

"For how long?"

"All winter—since the last summer season."

"Hadn't it been inspected several times with the idea that Morley's body might be there?"

"Yes—in a way. Officers looked through the windows but such a search was of course perfunctory. The windows were nailed down on the inside, the doors locked and Mr. Morley had the only key. No one at that time felt he had the right to enter the cottage by force since there was no evidence that a crime had been committed. The cellar, which was entered through an outdoor entrance, was subjected to search and when one could see in every room through the windows and there was nothing unusual to be seen, no further attempt was made to enter the cottage. That's why. Mrs. Morley was not pressed for permission to enter the place."

"If there was nothing seen at these examinations of the cottage prior to your discovery of the body, why was Mrs. Morley so afraid?"

"I really don't know—a presentiment of what she would find, perhaps."

"If Mr. Morley had the only key, how did you and Mrs. Morley intend to enter the cottage?"

"She intended to break in."

"Did she do that?"

"No. When we arrived at the cottage we found one of the windows up. I entered through it and found Mr. Morley's body in a bed in a terrible state of decomposition."

"Were the doors locked?"

"Yes."

"Rather strange that?"

"We thought so," replied LaVell as he fidgeted a little.

"Did you find the key to the cottage in Morley's clothes?"

"No. The next day some children who were wading in the lake found it."

"That's rather strange, too, don't you think?"

"I hadn't thought so."

"Do you think a suicide would enter the cottage, lock the doors, open a window, go down to the lake, throw the key away and then crawl back through a window and kill himself? If he were that meticulous about the details of his death, don't you think he would have put the window down after he entered the cottage the second time—perhaps even nailed it again?"

"I don't know. A man committing suicide might do anything. The very fact that he takes his own life is queer."

"Did it occur to you that he might have been killed—murdered—and that his body was placed in the cottage? It seems to me the facts justify that conclusion. Whoever placed his body in the cottage opened the doors with Morley's key and then placed the body in the cottage. They locked the doors while they were arranging the suicide stage. A window was raised—say on account of stench from the body. Or it might have been the intention of the murderers to close the window and then something frightened them at their task and they forgot it in their flight. Going by the lake one of them realized that the incriminating evidence was upon him and threw the key into the lake. Is that likely?"

"We thought of murder, gave it consideration, but there was no motive. There was a motive for a suicide. Morley's peculations at the bank furnished that. He realized that the bank examiners were coming soon and that he would be discovered. Why, the gun that was found beside his body was one that had been in his cage at the bank for years. Granting that a few happenings are hardly compatible with suicide, we have all felt that the major factors pointed to it, however."

"Have you the gun?"

"Yes."

"May I see it?"

"Certainly."

LaVell left them for a moment to return shortly with a revolver which he handed to Wilbur. The criminologist examined it closely.

"It's a Colt .32 caliber," said Wilbur, as he broke it and examined the chambers. "This is the way it was when you found it?" He held the barrel toward the light and peered through it. As he did so he covertly removed two of the cartridges and concealed them in his hand.

"It is as it was when it was picked up," answered LaVell.

"There are two cartridges missing."

"Oh no! Those are here—I mean the empty shells. I simply neglected to replace them in the gun."

"Morley was shot twice?"

"Twice. Once through the head and once through the heart."

"That's rather strange, isn't it?"

"Leading authorities say it can be done by a suicide."

"I am aware of the fact. It is startling. Did you recover the bullets?"

"No, we made no effort to secure them. It was the consensus of opinion that nothing would be gained by such a procedure. Besides there was a terrible stench from the body. The weather for a few days previous had been excessively hot. No human could stand it to be around it long. It was terrible. It was all that I could do to place it in a proper receptacle for burial."

"Still you were able to take the clothes from the body after you found it, were you not?" Wilbur asked naively.

LaVell reddened considerably. His face twitched, he shifted uneasily in his chair and stammered.

"Yes," he finally replied as he caught hold of himself. "But the odor was very much more pronounced after I removed the clothing. In my excitement, too, I might have been insensitive to odors at first. You understand."

"Just why did you remove the clothing?"

"I wasn't sure that it was Morley. I was trying to identify him."

"How did you expect to do it?"

"Well, from things in the clothing. Morley wore a suit I had never seen him have on before, so the clothing gave no clue. Then there were scars upon his body, an operative scar on the abdomen especially which his wife told me would clearly establish his identity."

"Did you find the scars?"

"No. When I had removed all of his clothing except the underwear I could go no further. The odor and condition of the body was so bad at that point that it was beyond human endurance and I desisted in the attempt."

"What did you do with the clothing you took off?"

"I burned it."

"Why?"

"It was of little consequence and was certainly something no one would like to lug around."

"Where did you burn it?"

"Am I to understand I am under a cross examination?"

"No, Mr. LaVell. I am only trying to get at a few facts. If you do not choose to answer my questions you need not. If you do not care to tell me where you burned the clothing, would you be kind enough to tell me what kind of a suit Mr. Morley had on at the time of his death? I believe you said he wore one you had never seen him wear."

"It was a gray tweed."

"LaVell, you're lying."

"Well, if you know so much about it, why ask me?"

Wilbur did not answer. Instead he reached in his pocket and brought forth the shank buttons. He handed the one he had picked up in the boat house to LaVell.

"Is that a button from Morley's blue serge suit?" he asked after a few moments of suspense.

"It is not a button from the suit he had on when found dead," LaVell answered.

"Well, possibly you're color blind. Maybe these other two buttons will freshen up your memory and give you more of an idea of color," said Wilbur as he passed the other two buttons to the undertaker. "I sifted these out of the ash pile behind what was once the cottage where you burned the clothing." LaVell looked at the evidence and laughed. "That's good! You're clever, Wilbur. Real clever! But I didn't burn the clothing behind the cottage. I burned it in the basement. I never saw these buttons nor any blue suit."

"You're clever at answering questions also. Of course one could sift the contents of the cellar but I hardly think it necessary. Where is the corpse?"

"The corpse is in the morgue."

"May I see it?"

"No, sir. That is impossible. It is in an hermetically sealed casket."

"My dear Mr. LaVell, you have been very courteous so far and I am sorry to cause any inconvenience but I must see the remains of the late Mr. Morley. Unless you desire to accommodate me I am afraid I shall have to invoke the aid of the court. I am going to view the remains. That is certain. Mr. Morley, from evidence in my hands, did not die in a gray tweed suit. He was killed in a blue serge."

"Sir!" said LaVell arising. "Do you mean to insinuate that I have lied? Do you mean to infer that I am in collusion with a murderer? Get out of my funeral parlors! Don't harass the dead. You won't in my place. You're positively insulting. Try and get a court to uphold you, you lowdown Keystone detective. You're funny! You can't come into this county and browbeat your way about. Men have been killed for less than you insinuate. They have hung people of your stripe around here. You insinuating pup!"

"Now listen, Mr. LaVell," replied Wilbur. "Save your epithets for someone who will appreciate them. I've handled more murder cases than you ever dreamed of burying. I know what I'm doing. Now that you've asked me to secure court aid I'm going to tell you something. I'm going to do it. I'm not going to fool with any county court either, where a seventh grade attorney makes everyone say his prayers to the political harlot. I'm going clear over all of that. Besides a post mortem of Morley, I'm going to have one of Mrs. Morley. We'll see who holds the cards. I'm going to take Eugene Morley out of the forty-five dollar casket you have probably put him in and learn the truth. And get this: no lay coroner is going to do the job."

Pierre LaVelle at that moment would have made an excellent model of the statue of Fear, as he clutched at himself, tried to be brave and put on a front. But a culprit never has the stamina of an innocent man. He cringed, gulped and stammered. Haughton and Wilbur arose.

"I am sorry, Mr. LaVell," said Wilbur. "I must see the remains of Eugene Morley and intend to do so. Your trouble is my sorrow. I thank you deeply for every courtesy you have shown."

"Get the hell out of my funeral parlors," yelled LaVell.

"I thank you," Wilbur said once more. "We'll be seeing you."

And then Lyman K. Wilbur left the funeral parlors of Pierre LaVell with his friend Jack Haughton.

CHAPTER VI

"COON HOLLOW"

"I AM CERTAINLY GOING to leave no stones unturned," Wilbur stated emphatically as he and Haughton left the funeral parlors. "I am going to have Eugene Morley posted. I am positive that a murder has been committed."

"There's no doubt of it in my mind," answered Haughton. "What's the next move?"

"I must secure permission to take Eugene Morley's body out of LaVell's casket."

"How are you going about it?"

"We must first find the Western Union office. I want to send a wire to the Governor. There's going to be action. The Bankers' Indemnity will see that there is. I'll wire them also and they will bear down on the Governor if it's necessary. No peanut politicians are going to shunt my inquiry. It's not going to be hushed up. There will be no monkey wrenches thrown into the machinery. I'm going to the roots of this affair no matter how far I have to go."

They climbed into Haughton's car, backed from the curbing and drove to the Western Union office. Telegrams were dispatched in order—one to the Governor and one to the Bankers' Indemnity.

"That's that," said Wilbur as he dashed off the last word to the Indemnity company and paid for the wires. "Now I believe I want to interview Mr. Fallows—sort of a social call rather than a questioning, just to get an insight into his character. You know where his office is, I presume."

Haughton pulled his car up in front of the legal luminary's office a few moments later.

"That is Mr. Blackstone's office," Jack remarked as he pointed to a front office in the second story of a frame building which was in a bad state of repair. "From the exterior you can readily perceive that he is one of the legal lights."

They alighted from the car and sought Mr. Fallows' office. Now Ambrose Fallows' office was nothing to make even a common pettifogger feel jealous about. A long dusty table graced the reception room upon which were magazines of the year before. A few straight backed chairs sat in confusion about the room. Two overly filled chewing tobacco boxes served as spittoons and sat on the floor at either end of the table. The windows were dirty; the curtains frayed and full of coal smoke and dirty black cobwebs hung from the ceiling. There was a picture of Abraham Lincoln on one wall and another of Noah Webster on another. On some shelving in disorder were almost a score of law books, musty, moldy and antiquated. One could see by glancing around that Ambrose was a big bright example of a prosperous attorney—one who rarely needed counsel. He relied on personality. This he had. He could make a widow sign before the corpse was cold. He had a knack. His practice ran to the settlement of estates, difficulties, and divorce. He seldom took a case to court. "Settle out of court" was his good advice to all clients, and Ambrose nearly always managed to pocket the settlement. Into his office stepped Wilbur, closely followed by Haughton. A sallow faced maiden lady of at least forty summers met him.

"Is Mr. Fallows in?" asked Wilbur.

"Yes, sir," replied the lady who had crossed up in her mating period. "He's busy just at present."

"Will he be engaged long?"

"I don't think so. Won't you sit down and wait?"

"Thanks."

Wilbur and Haughton sat down in two of the straight backed chairs. The girl, or middle-aged woman, entered Fallows' private office.

"You'd think she'd tidy this joint up a bit, wouldn't you?" asked Wilbur as he noted the room in detail.

"These small town offices are all this way, I've noticed. It's an heritage of the past, I guess. You don't dare look too prosperous in a poor community. I don't believe old Fallows would permit it."

The door opened into Fallows' private office and a tall well-dressed man came out. He cast a rather nasty look at the two men in the reception room and passed out.

"Who was that?" whispered Haughton. "Do you know him? He had a shoulder holster on. I got a squint at it."

"Oh, Finlay!" Fallows called as he opened the door of his private office and looked out. There was no answer. "Guess he's gone," Fallows said and closed the door again.

"I don't know the fellow personally but I've heard of him. I wouldn't have known if he hadn't called him," Jack whispered in answer to Wilbur's question. "It was Bob Finlay. He's supposed to be a rum runner."

"Ho hum!"

"He must have gotten into a jam."

"Either that or else he just received his orders." The elderly miss came out of the office at this juncture. She glanced at them.

"Mr. Fallows will see you now," said she.

Wilbur and Haughton arose to enter Fallows' private office.

"Be seated, gentlemen," importuned Fallows as he waved them to some chairs in front of his desk. "What can I do for you?"

"Mr. Fallows, I am an investigator for the Bankers' Indemnity Company," said Wilbur and he turned to Jack. "This is Mr. Haughton, a personal friend of mine who is summering at Ramona Lake."

"Glad to know you both," answered Fallows.

"I would appreciate it very much if I could have a few words with you."

Ambrose picked at his *pince nez* glasses, sucked in his breath and answered, "All right. What's on your mind, Mr. Wilbur?"

"You are a director in the Citizens' Trust, I understand."

"Yes, sir," replied Mr. Fallows. "A very trustworthy institution."

"When amply protected from absconders," Wilbur remarked pointedly.

"We pay our premiums promptly."

"Well, I don't care to discuss the solvency or insolvency of your bank, Mr. Fallows. I am only interested in it as it concerns the death of Eugene Morley. In spite of the suicide verdict I have made some discoveries which lead me to believe that Morley was murdered."

"My dear man, you must be a super-sleuth. It seems to me it has been definitely proven that Morley committed suicide."

"Definitely?"

"It would appear to be a clearly established fact. The authorities have accepted the theory."

"Well, Mr. Fallows, sometimes people call themselves authorities when they are really doing the bidding of someone else. I have found officers of the law who owed obligations to others and who had to do as these other people dictated. I have just interviewed your coroner. He tells me that Eugene Morley had on a gray tweed suit when found. I have almost indisputable proof that he wore a blue serge."

"Who said he had a gray suit on?"

"Your coroner."

"He's wrong. He wore a blue suit the day he disappeared. I never saw him wear gray in my life."

"How do you know?"

"I saw him the day he disappeared. He wore a blue suit. I remember it clearly."

"Well, someone is wrong. You tell me he wore a blue suit; LaVell tells me he had on a gray suit, and the tailor Felix Simon says that Morley had a deep aversion for blue and never wore the color. Of course I realize that he could have changed his mind about the color between the time of his disappearance and the discovery of his body. The color of the suit is of importance. But to get back to the death. I know Morley was killed. But who killed him?"

"I don't believe it. No one killed him. He killed himself."

"Well, you have it your way and I'll have it mine—until I prove that you are wrong. I'm not up here to argue. I just thought you might be able to help me a little on the case. Would you take a little nip of some good liquor with me, Mr. Fallows—just so we'll feel sociable?"

"I never refused but once," replied Fallows, whose dry face actually gave way to a smile. "But I didn't understand the man's language."

"How would a little Coon Hollow strike you, Mr. Fallows?" asked Jack as he produced a bottle from his hip pocket.

"Coon Hollow!" exclaimed Fallows. "That's Canadian."

"Sure it's Canadian," answered Jack. "I got this from a revenue officer who is hot on the trail of bootleggers operating about here."

"I'll take a small portion," said Fallows, as Jack poured a drink in the screw cup that fit over the cork of the bottle.

"That's very good," said Fallows after the drink. "Nice and mellow."

"I thought it was," answered Jack as he poured and passed a drink to Wilbur.

"Are your county officers O.K.?" asked Wilbur after his swallow. "They're not liable to be mixed up in a liquor racket?"

"Absolutely O.K.," Fallows answered. "Any officer in this county."

"Well, tell me where all the Coon Hollow comes from in this county. It seems to be plentiful. One can get it most any place. Morley's cottage was loaded with this stuff."

"What?"

"Eugene Morley's cottage was loaded with Coon Hollow. Besides that, there is a secret passage from the Morley cottage to the boat house at Baker's Landing. It looks very much as if Morley and some other people were illicitly trafficking in liquor." Wilbur watched Fallows closely, expecting him to betray himself by some facial expression. The lawyer disappointed him, however, and never so much as batted an eye. His flinty face remained immobile.

"What you tell me is of interest," Fallows replied. "Somehow I have always felt that Morley was engaged in an illicit business. If he was murdered it was probably done by someone who was interested with him in that business."

"You may be correct," replied Wilbur. "Morley was not a lone wolf."

"Well, I am certain I can shed no light upon the subject."

"Isn't it a fact that you are sort of a political czar in these parts?"

"Oh, I don't know. That's been said. But really I haven't any power. I'm in politics, of course, but—well, anyone gets a kick out of it."

"Doesn't it seem strange to you that Morley could operate with impunity over a long period of time without local protection?"

"If he did, yes. But I reckon it could be done. You know we country cusses aren't as suspicious as you city fellows."

"You're very intimate with Mr. Tully, aren't you?"

"Oh yes! I probably know Webb as well as anyone. I've been associated with him in business most of my life."

"Do you know anything about his financial condition?"

"He's pretty well off."

"Wasn't he in the hole pretty much a couple of years ago?"

"I guess he was. The casket business was pretty rotten for a while."

"It picked up in rather a startling fashion, didn't it?"

"The business suddenly took on a phenomenal growth. It grew by leaps and bounds. I've a little stock in the company so I happen to know the inside."

"I suppose LaVell buys his caskets direct from Tully, doesn't he?" asked Wilbur dryly.

"He'd hardly buy out of town," replied Fallows, unmoved by Wilbur's question.

"Would you have another drink of Coon Hollow?" asked Wilbur and turning to Jack said, "Pass the drinks."

Fallows took the drink which Jack poured, held it toward the light a moment from habit and then drank it.

"Would you say that was genuine or a clever fake?" asked Wilbur.

"It tastes genuine," replied Fallows. "Though one never knows these days. Labels and bottles are duplicated very easily."

As he spoke, the poker face of Ambrose Fallows never changed in expression. Wilbur had gained little if anything from his interview. Fallows was not a man to be easily trapped. Wilbur ceased to point any further remarks at the liquor business and returned to the subject of Morley.

"You say that Mr. Morley wore a blue serge suit the day he disappeared?"

"As I remember it," replied Fallows who was astute enough to cover up any slip which he might have made. "Of course it is possible that he wore gray."

"But I thought you said your attention was called to the blue serge. Didn't you say that you remembered it clearly?"

"Perhaps I did say that and perhaps I was wrong. You know and I know from contact with cases that no two men will give the same account of anything. It's that way with Morley's wearing apparel. I remember it as blue, the coroner as a gray. It's quite possible that the man wore neither color. He might have worn a brown suit."

"Memories are very deceptive," Wilbur replied. "Both you and LaVell saw the clothing Morley had on when last seen alive. You say he wore blue and LaVell says he wore gray. Felix Simon, the tailor, says he never wore blue. I know there was a blue suit on his dead body when it was found. Stick to the blue, Mr. Fallows. It was a very good guess."

"Somebody is wrong."

"Somebody is right. However I'll take up no more of your time. I'm very glad to have met you and will see more of you," said Wilbur as he terminated the interview.

On the street again Wilbur spoke to Haughton. "Not much out of Fallows," said he. "I didn't expect anything. I really wanted to study the man. I think I have a very good idea of him too. He'll bear watching. He measured his words carefully before speaking. The blue suit worries him. He said blue in the first place to agree with me. Later, after the liquor questioning, he became suspicious of everything and hedged on the color. His actions tell me that he knows more than he has told or will tell. The undertaker knows more than Fallows. This murder is a whole lot bigger than it appears on the surface. Now let's go to the Citizens' Trust. After seeing Fallows I feel I'd like to get an impression of Tully."

Together they entered the Citizens' Trust. Mr. Tully was cooped up within an enclosure, and a brass sign upon a flat top desk proclaimed the fact that the occupant was Webb Tully, the bank's president.

Mr. Tully was unoccupied when they entered and Wilbur passed through a low swinging gate into the president's place of conference, closely followed by Haughton.

"I am Mr. Wilbur, an investigator for the Bankers' Indemnity," said Wilbur and he immediately laid his credentials upon Mr. Tully's desk. "I'm investigating the Morley case."

"Oh yes," returned Tully as he drew up two chairs. "Mr. Fallows just telephoned that you were in the city. Won't you sit down?"

"This is Mr. Haughton," said Wilbur.

"I'm very glad to make your acquaintance, Mr. Haughton," said he as he shook hands with Jack.

"Now, Mr. Tully," Wilbur began after seating himself. "Just what can you tell me about the Morley case?"

"A dreadfully unfortunate thing," replied Tully. "And his wife's death, too. Her death was really more unfortunate than his. Death by fire I have always imagined to be a terrible thing. Well, gentlemen, I don't know what to say. The bank was short two hundred thousand dollars, as you no doubt know, and Morley's books show that he defalcated. We don't know where it went. It is simply gone. We've checked brokerage houses, race tracks, the grain exchange houses— everything in fact. But there's no trace of the money. We have diligently sought out those places where such money usually goes but with no result. It's gone, that's all. But in that connection I can probably tell you something which you have not yet learned. It's a peculiar coincidence."

"Oh God!" exclaimed Wilbur and Jack laughed outright.

"What's the matter?" inquired Tully.

"Nothing. Go on," answered Wilbur. "A coincidence is something that is hard for me to swallow and just lately I've swallowed several."

"Well, this is one. Mrs. Morley's uncle just left the bank a few moments ago. There is no trace of the fifty thousand dollars Mrs. Morley collected from the insurance company for her husband's death. It has been swallowed up just the same as the bank money—there's no trace of it. She cashed the check and the money disappeared. The uncle, the only living relative of Morley and his wife, thought she might have put it in the bank. It's not here and a check up of all the surrounding banks reveals no trace of it."

"Hum! That's interesting," replied Wilbur. "It's a motive for Mrs. Morley's murder. And you say the Morleys had no other living relative?"

"None whatever."

"Hum! Well, Mr. Tully, there seems to be a great number of strange happenings connected with this case or cases. Did you ever know that Eugene Morley was interested in the traffic of illegal liquor?"

"No, sir! It seems impossible. He applied himself to the bank too closely."

"I won't contradict you on that score. The evidence proves conclusively that his application was perfect," laughed Wilbur. "But nevertheless he was in the great American business clear up to his neck."

"I can't believe it."

Wilbur then told Tully of his discovery of the liquor cache and the tunnel. He watched the banker's reaction to his account closely. He was confident after his recital that Tully was uneasy.

"You're interested outside of the bank, aren't you, Mr. Tully?" the criminologist went on.

"Oh, in a number of things."

"How's the casket business?"

"Better," replied Tully with a grin. "The home undertaker bought two, you must remember."

"I'm serious, Mr. Tully. The casket business is very good, isn't it?"

Webb Tully hardly knew how to take Wilbur. He was very uneasy. "Oh, it's very good, Mr. Wilbur," Tully replied.

"It's a great deal better than it was a couple of years ago?"

"Oh, much better. You must know that I almost failed two years ago."

"I believe someone did mention that fact. You've a wonderful new home, haven't you—a Rolls-Royce and independence now?"

"Yes, a kind of shack. Real nice, but you know how people exaggerate."

"A man in my business always notices how people talk. The casket business must have become a bonanza."

"A very good investment after the usual manufacturers' vicissitudes," replied Tully as he passed a box of cigars which he pulled from a desk drawer.

"No, thanks," replied Wilbur. "But I would appreciate it greatly if you could tell me where I could get some real good bonded liquor. My tongue is about to flatten out upon the floor."

"I wouldn't know where to procure any, I am sure," replied Tully as he replaced the box of cigars after Jack had also declined to take one. "I understand there's plenty of the other kind—moonshine and the like."

"You wouldn't know where I could get some Coon Hollow?" Wilbur watched Tully closely.

"I don't know where you could procure a drop of good or indifferent liquor," replied Tully and Wilbur's close scrutiny of the man revealed nothing. "I don't use the stuff myself."

"You don't know anything more concerning Morley—anything which might aid me in this case?"

"I don't know that I do. Morley committed suicide and the money vanished. That's really about all the information anyone possesses. Up to the time of his disappearance the cashier had the respect of everyone. We never suspected him of any wrongdoing. It's a strange case."

"Well, for the argument's sake we'll grant that Morley did commit suicide. How do you explain the death of Mrs. Morley and the disappearance of the insurance money?"

"Her death was accidental. The money probably burned up with her clothing."

"Do you think a woman would go to that cottage at a late hour of night carrying fifty thousand dollars?"

"She might. Women do peculiar things. As a banker I have noticed they are far from being careful with money— especially insurance money."

"It's my theory that someone killed them both. Whoever killed Morley killed his wife."

"You still believe it is murder?"

"Most assuredly. There's something else that I wanted to ask you about. I almost forgot it. Do you recall the color of the suit Morley wore the day he disappeared?"

"Let me think!" replied Tully and after a few moments he said, "As I recall it he had on a gray suit. I'm almost positive of that."

"Gray? It wasn't blue?"

"Oh no, it couldn't have been blue. Morley had an aversion to blue. I don't believe I ever saw him wear a blue suit."

"That's what his tailor told me," replied Wilbur as he showed the three shank buttons to Mr. Tully and explained, "Those buttons were on Morley's clothes when he died."

Tully picked the buttons up and examined them. "Well, they may have come from the suit that Morley had on when he died, but I doubt it," said Tully as he handed the buttons back to Wilbur. "I've known Morley ever since he came to Summitville and I never saw him wear a blue suit. He was partial to gray. You'll notice such peculiarities in a man when you're closely associated with him day in and day out, year in and year out."

"Thanks, Mr. Tully, for your information," said Wilbur as he and Jack arose. "I don't believe you can aid me any more than you have. I surely appreciate what you have told me."

"Don't mention it. Good-by, gentlemen," replied Tully. "Don't hesitate to see me again if there's anything I can do to help you."

Leaving the Citizens' Trust Jack was the first to speak. "Not much satisfaction there," said he.

"Not much! And I'm beginning to wonder if the button clue isn't one of those numerous false clues that slip into a murder case. I've about lost my confidence in it. The tailor and Tully both say Morley would not wear a blue suit. LaVell and Tully say he wore gray. Fallows says he wore a blue suit the day he disappeared. I'm certain the lawyer was just attempting to agree with me, though. And why should he? That looks suspicious. Tully knows more than he has told. Do you know I'm beginning to think the entire Citizens' Trust was in on the gutting process? That doesn't necessarily mean they were in it together, either. Separately each one was taking funds from the bank. Morley was probably in the deepest and ran away from his crime. When he did so the others saw a chance to shift their thefts upon him. He became the goat for the bunch."

"Then you think he did suicide?"

"Oh no. I still think he was murdered. But I don't believe the actual peculation had anything to do with his murder. More and more I am of the opinion that he was murdered for another reason. To my mind his liquor dealing furnished the motive for his murder. Whoever was associated with him became afraid that the liquor business would be discovered when Morley was caught as a defaulter. They sealed his lips. That also explains Mrs. Morley's death. She was put out of the way to still her lips. She knew who Morley's associates were. She met them at the cottage to talk matters over, supposedly. She went to her death instead. The killer or killers took the insurance money."

"You still feel Mrs. Morley was murdered in spite of the fact that she showed no marks of violence?"

"A poison."

"Then you've given up the theory that LaVell was implicated?"

"Oh no! Not by a jugful. But your questioning reminds me: don't let me forget I want a toxicological examination of Mrs. Morley. That must be done after we get through with Morley's body. Don't let me forget it. It's a hunch, nothing more, but it wouldn't surprise me to learn that Mrs. Morley received a subtle poison in a glass of Coon Hollow."

"That's an idea. But who would do it?"

"Just who would do that, most likely, knowing what you do?"

"Pierre LaVell. He was out here with Mrs. Morley when the body of Morley was found and he was the last one to see her the night or morning she died."

"Who else?"

"Ambrose Fallows."

"Right again. You really do have ideas. There's nothing directly against Fallows but I can see you feel the same about him as I do."

"LaVell is the key."

"And now going back to those puzzling shoeprints. Whom has your wife been intimate enough with—to the extent that they could ascertain the fact that she wears her shoes off as she does?"

"God, Wilbur, I don't know. She's not been that intimate with anyone that I know of. And how anyone could duplicate her glove I haven't even the remotest idea. There's that damned coincidence again."

"I don't think it is a coincidence. I think there is only one woman who wears her shoes off that way."

"You can't—you don't mean that Alice—?"

"No, no. Hell, no!"

"But—I don't get you."

"Don't try to, Jack. This is too deep for a layman. The game is too intricate. It may be too big for a criminologist. Let's go down to the Western Union office and see if there is any word for me. Forget the shoes and the glove."

"All right, Wilbur," Jack answered. "But you're away ahead of me. I don't know any more about it than I do about a game of chess and I can't tell a knight from a pawn."

At the Western Union office Wilbur found an answer to his wire. The necessary authority would be forthcoming to perform a post mortem upon Eugene Morley. A representative of the state commission of safety would be in Summitville the next morning as an aid also. The criminologist read the telegram and expressed his satisfaction.

"Now our good friend LaVell may cry and sob," said he as he pocketed the wire. "We'll be able to view the results of his handiwork. I think it will be interesting. And now is there anything else that we want to do before returning to the cottage?"

"It's all up to you. I've no grasp of this affair at all," replied Haughton.

"I'm entirely different," returned Wilbur. "I've more grasps than an octopus but I don't know which grasp is correct. I think of several things to do but we'll pass them up until something further develops. I have found that if you go too fast in one of these murder things you get twisted up terribly, whereas a slow deliberate pace is conducive to results. We'd better go out to the cottage. I'll try and digest what I have assimilated."

CHAPTER VII

DYNAMITE!

AFTER SECURING THE GROCERIES which Alice had noted as necessary upon a piece of paper, Wilbur and Haughton climbed into Jack's machine. They headed down Main Street and turned right upon the road which led to Ramona Lake. As they passed the office of lawyer Fallows, Wilbur looked upward. The hawklike features of the Summitville attorney were peering out of a window. To Wilbur it appeared that he was watching their course out of town. There seemed to be a sardonic grin on his wizened face. Or was he mistaken?

Beyond the city limits Jack stepped on the accelerator. The machine shot forward until the index of the speedometer pointed to sixty odd miles per hour. The minds of both men were on the mystery. Wilbur's more than Jack's. They were probably out five miles from Summitville and approaching the bridge which spanned the Prairie River when Jack suddenly put on the brakes. Those mechanical devices fairly screamed. The car swerved right and left. Wilbur pitched forward and grabbed the edge of the door tightly.

"What the—?" cried Wilbur and then as the car finally came to a stop without overturning, Jack said, "Look ahead! God, that was close!"

Wilbur straightened back in his seat and looked ahead. There was no bridge across the Prairie River. They both alighted from the machine and walked to the edge of the river where one end of the bridge had rested. The bridge structure lay in the stream, a twisted mass of wreckage.

"Dynamite!" exclaimed Wilbur after a casual inspection. "I thought I heard a detonation just after we left Summitville but your motor was purring so loudly I wasn't sure."

"That was for our benefit. Whoever did it knows how I drive. They figured we would go hurtling into the river," replied Jack.

"There's not a soul here yet, so it couldn't have been so long ago."

"It makes me anxious about Alice."

"Hum! I never thought of that. And this might not have been done to kill us, come to think of it. It might have been done to delay us. After doing this they wouldn't stop when it came to harming her. The murderers around here seem to have no compunction about killing a woman. Turn around. How far is it to the lake now?"

"The other way around it is all of fifteen miles."

"Well, let's go! Step on it. God knows when anyone will be coming from Ramona Lake who might carry us onward even if we were able to cross the river."

They crawled back into Jack's car and he turned it around with a roar. It streaked backward down the road.

"Someone in Summitville is at the bottom of that," said Wilbur loudly as the telephone poles at the side of the road seemed to telescope one another. "LaVell! Fallows! Tully! Maybe all three."

"Yes, and if they would do that they were capable of executing the Morley murders. The fiends! I was so abstracted coming down the road that we almost fulfilled their desire. Four wheel brakes certainly were a godsend to us. Well, my mind is thoroughly on the road now until we hit the cottage."

"Perhaps we were too hasty. Now that we're over the hysteria maybe we can reason. That might not have been meant for us at all."

"The hell it wasn't."

"There's no contractor in this county who is nursing a grudge? It might have been done by someone who got a bad break. I noticed that was a new bridge. You know grafting commissioners could have let the bridge contract with partiality. And from the little I've learned of the Fallows-controlled outfit, that might happen."

"It might be the result of a contractor's grudge, but I don't believe it," answered Jack, whose eyes were glued on the road. He came to a corner, turned and then resumed, "That bridge was blown up to get you and me. Either that or it was blown up to delay us."

"Don't take it too seriously, old man," answered Wilbur. "Wait until we find out. I think Alice is safe and sound."

Jack was not so sure, however.

"Well, if someone was clever enough to point the finger of suspicion at her through a pair of shoes they might be clever enough to do something else. Hell, but this car is slow," he said.

Wilbur looked at the speedometer. It was doing seventy-eight miles an hour. Jack was taking curves at almost top speed, making turns at an ungodly rate, and doing a reckless job of driving.

"Yes, it's crawling," replied Wilbur. "If you keep the speed you are now going you will do exactly what the destroyers hoped that the removal of the bridge would do."

"I guess you're right," said Jack as he slowed his pace.

"That's more like it."

The register dropped from seventy-eight miles an hour to forty-five.

"We're getting close anyhow," said Jack. "And from here on there's plenty of turns. This is the lake road now."

They soon passed Bakers Landing, coming in as they did by another route. A few moments later they pulled up in front of Haughton's cottage. There was no sign of life about and Alice never failed to meet Jack whenever he arrived. They hopped out in less time than it takes to tell it and made for the front door. It was locked.

"Good God!" cried Jack as he knocked loudly. "Alice! Alice!"

There was no answer.

"Let's go to the back," Jack suggested. "No!" answered Wilbur and with one smash of his fist he broke the glass in the front door. Not waiting to reach inside and turn the key they climbed in through the broken glass door.

"Alice! Alice!" cried Jack as they ran from room to room. There was no answer from her. Every room was searched. There was no trace of her.

"God, this is terrible, Wilbur," said Haughton as he sank into a kitchen chair. "Get me a drink. The bottle's in the cupboard."

Wilbur procured the bottle and gave Jack a drink. "Don't go on so, old man," he cautioned. "Don't get panicky. Maybe she just stepped out. Maybe she's gone to one of the neighboring cottages." Wilbur poured himself a drink. He needed it. He wasn't so sure about the disappearance of Alice. The thing might have a nasty angle. He hadn't forgotten the shoes and gloves. But the object!

"She never leaves the cottage except when she is with me," Jack answered. "Something is wrong."

"Well, anyhow, pull yourself together. Let's look around again and make sure she isn't here. Then we'll go outside and make some inquiry. We'll cover every cottage on the lake. She might have taken a notion to explore the tunnel. Maybe she went fishing."

"No, she cares nothing for the sport."

"Well, never worry, she'll turn up."

They searched the cottage thoroughly again.

"Yoo hoo!" a voice called from the outside just as they finished. Jack ran to the window and looked out. Coming up the road from the direction of Bakers Landing was Alice.

"Here she comes," yelled Jack.

He and Wilbur went out on the cottage porch. It was a great relief to see her.

"You're a couple of fine gentlemen," said she as she approached them. "I yelled myself hoarse when you passed Bakers Landing but you wouldn't pay the least attention."

"Sorry, but we didn't hear you," replied Jack. "Where on earth have you been? We've been worried sick. Someone blew up the bridge over the Prairie River and we had to detour. We came mighty near piling up in the river. We thought it might have been done to hold us up so the scoundrels that have officiated in these murders might harm you. When we arrived and you were not here you can imagine all the terrible things we thought."

"It was lonesome around here. And having you two around all the time made me detective minded. I just thought I'd stroll about a bit and see what I could pick up in the way of evidence."

"Any luck, Mrs. Haughton?" asked Wilbur.

"Well, I don't know," she replied, as she brought a hand forward which she had held behind her back. "But I found this lying in the grass near Bakers Landing."

Her hand held a .32 caliber Smith and Wesson revolver which she grasped at the end of the barrel.

"Oh God!" exclaimed Wilbur. "You didn't handle it?"

"Say, what kind of a dumb dick do you think I am?" asked Alice. "I suppose you think I've been playing with it, seeing whether it will fit my hand, or shooting it off. There's one thing I will say; it's not a coincidence. I didn't touch it except at the end of the barrel. Otherwise it's just as I found it."

"Great!" exclaimed Wilbur as she carefully transferred the weapon to his hands. "You're immense, Alice. Let's go. Get my paraphernalia out of my grip, Jack, and we'll go to work. We'll get the prints if there's any on it and after that we'll examine the gun."

All three trooped into the cottage. Jack laid out all of Wilbur's fingerprint material and Wilbur proceeded to take the prints. In no great time he secured what prints were on the handle.

"Well, there are the prints," said Wilbur as he finished. "I don't know whose they are but we have them in case we need them. Now I'll examine the gun."

Wilbur broke the weapon and removed the shells. Two had been fired.

"That complicates matters," he remarked. "Or else it makes the job easier."

He held the gun toward the light and looked down the barrel.

"Hum!" said he. "Right offhand I'd say this gun was fired at about the same time that the gun LaVell has was fired. I've got so used to the appearances that I don't even have to use a 'helixometer' any more." Looking up at Alice, he explained, "A helixometer is a periscopic tube and an arrangement by which the gun can be advanced and the tube rotated at the same time, enabling an examiner to cover the entire inside of a gun barrel as though he were looking directly at it. He can thus study the fouling, rust or whatever may be within the barrel. If my conjecture is true we have quite a little mess on our hands."

Wilbur examined the shells next. Two had been fired. "Two fired as in the gun which LaVell has!" he exclaimed as he picked up the gun again, suddenly examined it and remarked further, "The numbers have been filed off. A damn clever crook owned it. The gun didn't belong to an honest individual, that's sure, for honest individuals don't mutilate their weapons in that manner."

Laying one of the unfired shells from the gun which Alice had picked up aside, Wilbur dug deep in his pocket and pulled forth another. As he laid this shell beside the other one on the kitchen table he remarked, "I did a little sleight of hand performance at LaVell's undertaking establishment today and filched this cartridge from the gun which is supposed to have shot the bullets which killed Morley."

The two cartridges lying side by side looked identical. "Both have been made by the Peters Arms Company," said Wilbur.

"They are alike, aren't they?" asked Jack. "That ought to tell a tale."

"Not if they are alike," replied Wilbur. "I'm not at all sure that they are. In fact I hope they are not alike. We'll see."

Thereupon Wilbur took the lead noses from the cartridges and dumped the contents of the cartridges upon the table.

"Hum! Damn!" exclaimed Alice, and then collecting herself asked pardon for the assumption of Wilbur's pet expression.

"You see it, eh?" he asked.

"Sure I do," replied Alice.

"You'd make an excellent detective."

"What is it?" asked Jack as he looked dumbly at the small piles of shell contents.

"The powder!" cried Alice. "You dumbkopf."

"Oh yeah!"

"Sure!" exclaimed Wilbur as he pointed to each pile of powder in turn. "The cartridge from the gun which is supposed to have been used by Morley in the suicide is loaded with Ballistite smokeless powder. The cartridge from the gun which Alice found is loaded with black powder."

"I see it now. Well! Isn't that hot!" exclaimed Jack as he noticed the difference. "God, I'd never make a detective in a thousand years. I'm too slow."

"That's something. Don't think it isn't," replied Wilbur and casting his eyes towards Alice he added, "And but for you we wouldn't know it."

"Well, how about a little Coon Hollow for a change?" asked Jack.

CHAPTER VIII

GUN PLAY

THE REST OF THE DAY wore on. The trio in the cottage forgot the tragedies at Ramona Lake and indulged in a little recreation. They took a rowboat which Jack had acquired with his purchase of the cottage and went fishing. Alice rowed while Wilbur and Jack cast for bass. The day was a perfect one for a person with a president's tendencies. The bass had received no inhibition from the lake happenings and struck hard and frequently. As a result they returned to the cottage at dusk, the possessors of a fine fry. After the criminologist and Haughton had cleaned them, Alice did a fine job of frying. They sat down to their supper with a fisherman's appetite and proceeded to clean the platter.

"That dynamiting of the bridge preys on my mind, Wilbur," Jack finally remarked after appeasing his appetite with a third helping of fish. "That was meant for us."

"Oh, my dear boy," answered Alice. "Just as my absence from the cottage meant harm had befallen me. You are murder-case conscious. Everything that occurs from now on will have some connection with the Morley case, I suppose. It's a wonder to me you haven't supposed that the fish tasted funny—that they were poisoned for you and struck at your bait just because the Morley killers told them to. Come out of it."

"It's silly, I guess," Jack answered. "Maybe I am jumpy, but when one gets that way what can one do?"

"Buck up and forget it," replied Wilbur as he separated the bones from a piece of fish meat. "I know how you feel, though. I used to be that way a good deal and even get that way at times yet. You're jumpy, as you say. On a hard case shadows look like men to me, and men like shadows, and finally I get so bad that I imagine everything that happens has a bearing on the case I'm working on. It's nerves. You get over that largely in time but never entirely. The dynamiting of the bridge is probably as far away from the Morley case as Mars is from the earth. I still think it's a contractor's way of getting even with commissioners who wouldn't give him a break."

"It isn't being jumpy at all if you ask me," said Alice. "It's just too much Coon Hollow."

"All right, you two," replied Jack. "I'll get even with you. I've got one of my hunches. You'll find out I wasn't jumpy and that I didn't have too much Coon Hollow."

Wilbur was about to lift a forkful of fish meat to his mouth when there was a crash. The north window of the kitchen shattered into a million pieces and the light above the table went out.

"Drop to the floor quick," warned Wilbur. "Where are the guns, Jack?"

"Damn stupid, I'll say. They're in the other room on the table. I told you so," said Jack as he dropped to the floor.

"Lie still!" commanded Wilbur as he wriggled like a snake into the living-room. As he did so four or five more shots entered the kitchen from all angles.

Wilbur secured the guns, crawled back and gave one to Jack.

"Come on!" said he. "Let's go!" Directing his conversation to Alice he cautioned, "Stay where you are, Alice, and don't move."

By stealth Wilbur and Haughton left the kitchen by a rear door and edged their way around the south side of the cottage. They approached the front of the cottage in the shadow of the building. Gaining that perspective, Wilbur looked around a corner and saw a fleeing form close by the lake going down the lake road toward Bakers Landing. He leveled his revolver at the fleeing figure and fired.

"Come on Jack! There he goes," said he as he dashed forth from the cover of the cottage. Jack followed. The two had traversed about the first thirty feet in front of the cottage when a gun barked behind them.

"Down! Down!" shrieked Wilbur as the man who was fleeing down the lake road turned to fire. "We're pocketed."

Both of them fell prone. As Wilbur turned and twisted to find out where the shots came from in the rear, he saw that the firing was coming from the cellar of the Morley cottage. He saw a flash, raised his gun to aim at the spot where the flash came from but did not fire. A burst of flame issued from the Haughton cottage.

"Crack! Crack! Crack! Crack!" came the staccato bark from Haughton's cottage. Silence, and then a lone return shot came from the basement of the Morley cottage. A well directed shot from Wilbur towards the flash in the Morley cellar silenced everything. All the firing ceased. Slowly, carefully, Wilbur and Haughton made their way back to the cottage around the south side. They reentered it. Alice was standing a few feet from the window, doubled up, supporting her right arm. In her right hand she held an automatic.

"Are you hurt, Alice?" asked Wilbur, who entered first and noted her position.

"Slightly," she replied. "Not much though. That last shot from the cellar got me in the arm."

"Come in the bedroom," said Jack. "Let's see it." Jack took her into the bedroom where he could safely turn a light on. Wilbur remained on guard in the darkened kitchen. Jack closed the door, turned on the light and found with much relief that his wife's injury was only a flesh wound. No bones were broken. It bled profusely but that was all right. He cleaned it up and flooded the puncture with mercurochrome and covered it with sterile gauze and a bandage.

"God, that was a lucky break," said he as he put the first-aid kit away. "Why didn't you remain on the floor as we told you to do?"

"Oh, yeah!" replied Alice. "Well, if I had, you and Wilbur would both be good receptacles for embalming fluid at this instant. When you went out I crawled into the bedroom, got your automatic from under your pillow and returned to the kitchen. As I looked out of the window upon my return a form arose over the wall of the Morley cottage and the next thing I knew it was shooting at you. I shot at it through the shattered window four times and then my gun jammed. Next thing I knew I felt a sting in my right arm and something warm ran down it. I held my arm tight with my left hand and tried to get my arm to work. There was another shot. I saw the form in the Morley cellar disappear. And then you returned."

Jack turned the lights off in the bedroom and they returned to the kitchen.

"Is she injured badly?" Wilbur asked anxiously.

"It's only a flesh wound, luckily," replied Jack. "The bones are all intact. I swabbed it with mercurochrome and bandaged it."

"Slight injury or large, she'll have to be taken to a doctor," replied Wilbur. "She must have tetanus anti-toxin. No gunshot wound, however trivial, is to be fooled with. Furthermore I don't think this cottage is safe at all. Since the bullets I'm afraid the bridge tactics may be resumed."

"You think they might dynamite the place?"

"The fiends that are doing all this devilish work will stop at nothing. They're gone now, but when darkness comes in earnest and when they think vigilance has been relaxed they will appear again. It is their intention to annihilate us if they can. We evidently know too much."

"What do you suggest that we do?"

"Well, I suggest that we pack up our evidence and whatever you have of value and go to the Summitville House. We've got to go to Summitville anyhow so that Alice can receive medical attention."

"That's a splendid idea."

"Sure it's a good idea. We could watch all night and perhaps outsmart anyone who attempted to get in the cottage. We might forestall any serious shooting. But dynamite, nitroglycerine or pineapples could be hurled at us. There is ample evidence that we will be done away with if the thing is possible."

"Hadn't I better slip out and report this to the sheriff?" asked Jack.

"A waste of breath if you ask me," replied Wilbur. "It's probably already been done. That shooting was heard all up and down the lake. If the sheriff knew about it he'd only make a perfunctory examination and call the incident closed. No! Let it pass as an incident."

"Who was it?"

"I don't know. I'd like to examine those footprints along the lake but it's out of the question. It is too hazardous. I won't be able to do it in the morning either for I'll be too busy with LaVell."

"Well, if we are going let's get busy," said Jack. "You get your evidence and paraphernalia together while I pack up our important belongings."

It was barely an hour until the Haughtons and Wilbur were ready to abdicate the Haughton cottage on Ramona Lake. The grips, packages and essential articles were surreptitiously placed in the automobile under the cloak of darkness. The latter had fallen fast. With guns alert, they escorted Alice to the car and helped her inside. Jack climbed in behind the wheel and started the motor. It sounded like a train on the still night air. Wilbur jumped in beside Jack as the big car started down the short lane which led from the cottage to the lake road.

"Don't turn your lights on until you're on the lake road," Wilbur cautioned Jack. "And don't go toward Bakers Landing. It may be thirty miles to Summitville this way since the bridge is out but what matter? If we went toward the landing we might be ambushed since our attackers fled in that direction. Take it easy too. There might be another bridge out."

Jack made the lake road without any difficulty and turned to the left. He could follow the lake road without lights by driving slowly. This he did for a distance of a mile or so.

"I think you can safely turn the lights on now," said Wilbur. "We're quite a way from the cottage, no one seems to be following us and there's nothing to indicate that this escape has been watched."

Jack flashed on the lights and accelerated the car. Everyone felt easy at last.

"It's a long way to Summitville," said Jack as he lit a cigarette.

"Never mind. I'm constrained to believe the route would be too short had we gone by way of Bakers Landing," replied Wilbur.

"Oh yes, Lyman," said Jack. "I'd like to ask a question. Have you changed your mind about the Prairie River bridge, or do you still think that contractor is nursing his grudge?"

"No, I'm forced to believe that someone thinks dead men tell no tales."

"Well, things are getting exciting. You can't say that we don't have our little moments down here."

"And how!"

They sped along at a moderate rate of speed. The hum of the motor, the night air—everything was tranquil. And then all of a sudden there was a reverberation—a "boom" behind them. Wilbur leaned out of the car and looked back.

"There it went! The cottage!" said he. "They've blown it up. God! We just escaped in time."

"Oh!" shuddered Alice.

"If it was to be there's no use in crying over spilled milk," said Jack philosophically. "The dump didn't cost a fortune. Even if it wasn't insured, we are still alive. We should worry."

A few moments later Haughton headed the car eastward. All three could now see a lurid flame leaping skyward back on Ramona Lake.

"Oh say, did you bring the Coon Hollow?" asked Wilbur.

"Didn't I tell you I'd pack up all of our important belongings?" answered Jack.

CHAPTER IX

THE SHERIFF PAYS A CALL

THE TRIO, ALICE, WILBUR AND JACK, arrived in Summitville with no mishap. Alice was taken to a doctor immediately. The professional man redressed her wound and gave her anti-tetanus serum. He gave a good prognosis and called the wound trivial. After this attention they registered at the Summitville House and secured adjoining rooms. Jack parked his car on a side street which ran along one side of the hotel where there were no parking limitations. He and Wilbur carried all of their belongings to their rooms.

"I don't believe anyone will attempt to blow the hotel up," said Jack as he fished in his effects for the bottle. 'The damn thing has my nerves, though—what we've experienced. Send out for some ginger ale, Lyman. I know I need some dutch courage, moral support or whatever a little liquor does to a tattered nervous system. In fact a large copious draught isn't going to do me one bit of harm. I'm sure there's no sleep for me tonight anyhow."

"I'll just run out and get it myself," replied Wilbur. "I might get an earful on the explosions while I am out. I'll tell the clerk to bring a pitcher of ice water up."

Wilbur purchased the ginger ale at a drug store about a block from the hotel. Going and coming from there he passed numerous knots of men who were discussing the dynamiting of the Prairie River bridge and the Haughton cottage. The latter news had been relayed in faster than Wilbur expected. He stopped at one knot after another and lingered at the edges to get the conversation.

"It's just proof that Eugene Morley was murdered," said a spokesman in one group. "There's a smart city detective workin' on the case and he's been staying at that fellow Haughton's cottage. He's just picked up some evidence that's goin' to hurt somebody and they tried to knock him off."

"There wasn't no one in the cottage when it went up, was they?" some inquisitive listener asked.

"Nope," answered the spokesman. "Followin' the shootin' at the cottage, the Haughtons and this detective guy pulled out. Someone was tellin' me they pulled into the hotel a while ago."

"Close shave!" said someone else. "By cracky, I wouldn't want to be no detective."

"Oh, they'll get the guys that done the dynamitin'," the spokesman continued. "The sheriff's out at Ramona Lake now lookin' things over. He ain't so dumb."

"Only when Ambrose Fallows wants him to be," put in another party who evidently had some insight in the county situation. "I'm bettin' there ain't nothin' done about the whole thing. The county outfit will figure the shootin' to be a prank and the dynamiting an accident. This county needs a cleanin'."

At another group the speaker's voice was strangely familiar. When Wilbur got a good view of him he recognized the taxi driver who had taken him to Ramona Lake.

"This guy from New York is a damn keen head," the taxi driver was telling his audience. "I took him out to the Haughton cottage the night he came in. He found the booze in the Morley cottage and discovered the tunnel leadin' down to the lake. I'll bet some bootlegger took Morley for a ride and he's learned the detective's got his number. It's that old gag that dead men tell no tales."

"Yeah, I'll bet you're right too," put in a listener. "My sister works in the Western Union and there was a telegram came in today from the governor's office for this detective you're speakin' about. They're going to hold an autopsy on Morley in the morning. Whoever is guilty of killin' Morley knows the jig's up."

"Well, there's something that guy already knows or is about to find out that's got someone pretty nervous," the taxi driver went on. "They seemed hell bent on gettin' rid of him tonight when they used dynamite after failin' with a gun."

"Oh, I reckon the guy ain't scared none," put in another of the group. "He's been mixed up with regular he-gangsters where he came from. This Summitville stuff is just sort of a lark for him, I'll bet."

"Yeah, you can tell after talkin' to him that he's got guts," the taxi man extolled Wilbur, "An' damn my buttons if I don't think he's goin' to land Gene Morley's killer."

Wilbur grinned when he left this group to listen to others. The conversation of all the gatherings was similar. He learned nothing, except the divergent opinions, which were many.

Returning to the hotel he found company. The sheriff and the prosecutor were standing in the room. Jack introduced them.

"The sheriff has been out at Ramona Lake looking the ruins over," said Jack. "He came here to ask us a few questions. From what he has asked so far I gather the impression that he thinks we are to blame for the dynamiting."

"That's very likely," laughed Wilbur, as he set the ginger ale down. "I can hardly imagine anyone demolishing his home just for a pastime."

"Insurance, perhaps," the sheriff suggested.

"There was none on the building," replied Jack. "It ran out just before I purchased it and I neglected to take out a new policy. The cottage is a total loss."

"It might have been destroyed to conceal something. It strikes me funny that a New Yorker would purchase a cottage on this lake anyhow, so far away," replied the sheriff.

"Conceal what? Explain yourself," said Wilbur.

"Well, a *booze* operation for one thing," the sheriff suggested nastily. "I found plenty in the Morley cottage."

"That has nothing to do with the Haughtons, I assure you," replied Wilbur.

"Oh yeah!" replied the sheriff. "Then maybe you can explain why that property's recorded in his name, deeded over to him on the same date that the dynamited one is?" the sheriff interrogated in a caustic tone.

"Deeded to me? The Morley cottage? You're lousy," put in Jack. "I never bought anything but the cottage which was dynamited."

"Hum! That's slick, ain't it?" the sheriff said to the prosecutor. "It's a matter of record, ain't it?"

"It's on the books," the prosecutor acknowledged.

"Well, if it's on the books it's a damn trick," put in Jack. "I'll burn somebody plenty for that."

"Well, all I got to go on is the record," the sheriff went on. "And the record shows you're the owner of what was the Morley cottage. It's mighty funny one of your cottages is burned one night and the other blown up another night. And since finding out you owned the Morley cottage I ain't so sure Eugene Morley committed suicide. And I doubt that his wife met an accidental death. It appears to me there's a good reason for holdin' a first class post-mortem in the morning."

"Oh rot, sheriff," said Wilbur. "That's perfectly asinine."

"I ain't so sure about it," the officer of the law answered. "And grantin' you're Lyman K. Wilbur, that ain't provin' you ain't mixed up in a bootleggin' scheme either. You might 'a had a hand in the other stuff too. You was here the night Mrs. Morley burned. You wouldn't be the first lily to be caught in the liquor racket."

"Your theory is amazing," returned Wilbur in almost a rage. "It's so absolutely ridiculous it's too bad. You or somebody else think they are mighty clever. It is getting too hot for someone. It got hot today. The liquor racket and the Morley deaths are worrying someone. Somebody with a fast working mind planned a clever escape. Haughton here bought his cottage from Morley and he made a deed to him. After the discovery of the liquor and the tunnel, whoever was scared added all of Morley's adjoining property to that transfer, if the records at the court house are as you say they are. They thought to pin the thing on my friend—that and the deaths. Well, we'll see about it. It sounds clever, looks nice, and might work but I don't think so." Turning to Jack, Wilbur asked:

"Where's your deed, Jack?"

"I left the damn thing in the cottage," Jack answered in a crestfallen manner.

"Ha! Ha!" laughed the sheriff and winked at the prosecutor. "That's a good one. The deed's gone, Morley's gone, and the recording is all that is left to establish ownership of the property. That'll be hard to take."

"But we do not own the ground upon which the Morley cottage stood," put in Alice. "Somebody has changed the record."

"I'm afraid you'll have to let a court decide that for you, Madam," said the sheriff. "As the matter now stands, the property evidently belongs to you. But really I wouldn't worry about it as all we have against you is possession of liquor. Under the Burleson Act in this state the penalty for possession is only a thousand dollar fine and a year's imprisonment. Of course a new construction will be put on the Morley deaths. It remains to be seen whether you can be connected with them."

"Just a minute, sheriff," replied Wilbur. "You are a bit hasty and you had better slow down before you trip. The deed is gone—we'll admit that. Morley is dead—we'll admit that. We'll even admit that the record of the deed in the courthouse is as you say it is. In spite of everything you haven't proved anything."

"I don't quite get you," replied the officer.

"You wouldn't. Neither would the person with the clever brain who filled in the additional description of property on the record. The deed originally had a description of the cottage which was blown up and its grounds. Deeded by Morley in the first place, it was quite easy to add a description of the cottage which burned and the grounds which accompanied it. Morley is dead and couldn't come back to dispute it. His wife is also dead. It looks like there was no way of disputing it but there is. The additional description was added a considerable period after the record was first made. And if the record includes the Morley cottage and grounds I'll prove that it was added."

"I've heard you city detectives were pretty smart," replied the sheriff with a grin.

"The idea was very clever whosoever it was, but there are those little niceties of detection of which the man who alters documents does not know. Since you have been so zealous to run down the ownership of the Morley cottage, did you learn who tried to kill us? Who did the shooting?"

"No one except yourselves," replied the sheriff. "No one else about the lake saw anyone. It sounds like an excuse to blow the cottage up. That was clever too."

"Do you think one of us deliberately shot my wife?" asked Jack as he pointed to Alice's bandaged arm.

"A flesh wound no doubt. Yes, that would fit in well with your story," replied the sheriff.

"You certainly have a marvelous brain, sheriff," put in Wilbur. "With your skull cut down to fit it I earnestly believe you could get along very well with a peanut shell for a hat. Your brain is a wonder. It's a wonder you are able to think at all. Now, I've a little suggestion to make. You arrest any or all of us pronto. I'll guarantee that things will sizzle. Or you can wait until after the autopsy tomorrow and bring that court record to Summitville. I'll demonstrate conclusively that the document is false. If I don't you may immediately arrest one or all of us for conspiracy to violate the prohibition law. But I'll warn you before you do that, too. The trial may result in the conviction of somebody else. I'm not guessing, not surmising, and won't have to change any documents. Do you understand me?"

"No, I don't get you," replied the sheriff. "But if you can show me that the document has been tampered with I'd like to be shown. I'll not get out any warrants for any of you but right after the autopsy I'll be in Summitville with the record of that deed."

"See that you do that, sheriff," answered Wilbur. "I'll show you the document was changed and after the autopsy I think I'll be able to show you that Morley was murdered. I'll go further than that. I'll even venture a guess that I'll prove Mrs. Morley was murdered as soon as I can have a toxicologist examine her remains."

"That's an awful chunk to bite off," returned the sheriff as he and the prosecutor sought the door.

"Oh, yeah! Well, thank God, neither Mr. Haughton, his wife or myself will have to swallow it. Good night, gentlemen."

"Good night," returned the two officials.

Wilbur closed the door after the two county officers and shut the transom.

"Look and see if there is a fire escape on this fire trap and lock the windows," he ordered.

Jack examined them, reported there was no fire escape, and that the windows were locked securely.

"Give me a highball, quick!" said Alice. "I'm frayed. I need to relax."

"Me too, Lyman," said Jack, as he noticed Wilbur was starting to officiate. "First you had to dally on the street corners, and then the sheriff. I'm away behind."

"I need one myself," replied Wilbur as he made the drinks.

"Well, we're in a jam," said Jack as he picked up his glass. "Some dirty louse-bound rat has tampered with the record. I can't see how you're going to prove that the description of Morley's property was added. It looks to me like we're hooked."

"Never mind," returned Wilbur. "I said I'd prove it and I will. When the proper time comes I'll do it. Just at present allow me the pleasure of drinking this highball in peace. I certainly do admire Coon Hollow."

Alice downed her drink. "Now for a little much needed rest," she said. "If you two fellows are going to remain up I'll feel perfectly safe in bed."

"Do that, honey," replied Jack. "I know you are tired. You had hardly any sleep last night. I think everyone is entirely safe here but right at the present I couldn't sleep if I wanted to."

Alice bade Jack and Wilbur good night and retired to the next room. Wilbur sat deep in thought, rolling cloud after cloud of tobacco smoke toward the ceiling.

"Well, what's the dirt?" asked Jack after watching him some moments in silence.

"I'm trying to piece the jumbled mess together," the criminologist replied. "It's worse than any puzzle I ever ran across. There are so many leads, angles, motives and suspects that I hardly know where to begin. The attempts to kill us failed. Now an attempt is being made to railroad us to prison. It looks to me like Morley's partners in the illicit traffic of liquor reside right here in Summitville."

"They are desperate. I don't think they're pikers or engaged in a pikers' business," replied Jack. "They're men of importance and the business is too big to be given up easily. That's what prohibition has done—made criminals out of a large portion of the population."

"It's a great racket when properly engineered. To start it and carry it through on a large scale would require a large sum of money. Bank funds would be readily accessible to people within a bank—sufficient for such an enterprise. Might Morley have furnished the funds? Might a demand of his for a return of that money have caused his associates to kill him? Might he not have known that his appropriation was about to be discovered? He would be desperate in that case and if the money was not forthcoming he might have made threats which resulted in his death. Our knowledge of his involvement might have caused certain people to desire our disappearance."

"You mean Fallows and Tully?"

"That's just who I mean, together with the sheriff, the prosecutor, and other county officers. There may be even more in the racket. It might be a state-wide affair."

"Hum! Damn it! It looks like it but I can't see anything that connects any of them directly. It's all circumstantial evidence. That to me is just like a coincidence. And if any of them are involved, Pierre LaVell must be."

"I forgot him. He's under Fallows' thumb."

"It doesn't seem possible that so many supposedly respectable people could be involved in a thing of this kind and no actual proof against a single one."

"That's 'organization.' "

"Organization of that sort requires a master mind."

"And you've got it—Ambrose Fallows. That hawk-bill isn't on his wizened face for nothing and his skull is no chemocephalic one."

"Once you said you thought Morley's absconding had nothing to do with his murder."

"Pardon me! That might have been the impression I created. I meant his suicide."

"I'm only sure of one conclusion—we know too much or someone thinks we do. What's it about? The liquor business? Morley's death? Mrs. Morley's death? Or what have you?"

"We are probably given credit for knowing a lot more than we really do. We must be, for we both know that we have no positive information about anything."

"Does LaVell have to fit into this conspiracy?"

"Why separate him? He's undoubtedly connected with it."

"I am not so sure."

"Are you talking, Jack, or is it the Coon Hollow?"

"I am talking. LaVell may have been working a racket separate and distinct from the other."

"You think—"

"It has been rumored that he was thick with Mrs. Morley. She might have told him of Morley's insurance. They might have connived to kill Morley to secure the insurance. After that LaVell might have double-crossed Mrs. Morley. It's not improbable that he secured the insurance money and the two hundred thousand from the bank. It would be a neat trick."

"But the attempt against our lives? There were two people who shot at us. If your theory is correct LaVell had a confederate."

"He may have had."

"Who was that?"

"Search me! I don't know, as I said before. It's a Chinese puzzle. I'm at my wit's end. Instead of unraveling, the case gets worse."

"Never mind, it will unravel. It is always darkest just before dawn," said Wilbur as he poured himself a short "snifter" and laughed. "Don't forget I have three shank buttons, shoe prints, two evidently identical cartridges, but each charged with a different kind of powder—and a stuffed lady's glove. Say, Sherlock Homes used to solve tougher cases with less than that. Cheer up! That information is of some moment. Otherwise there wouldn't be this insistent demand for my demise."

"So far everything seems silly."

"Granted! Everything is too silly. That's the point. It gives me a theory—a silly theory. Tomorrow morning I'll know whether this is all a goofy mess or the pieces that make a crazy quilt. If my theory is proven right we have only started the case."

"What's the theory, Lyman? Tell me. I'll not laugh at it."

"No, I won't even give you a suggestion. It's too fanciful. If it proves out wrong I'd feel like a simp. And my deduction is absolutely childish."

"Well, if you even have a childish idea of this whole affair you have me bested."

"All of these so-called mysteries are simple. They are really not mysteries at all, once you get the hang of them. In every one all that is necessary is patience. You assemble your clues, look them over and pick upon the most promising one. In this you may err, for the one you think the most important may turn out worthless. But nevertheless that's the way you start your trip down the path of clues. One runs into another, some lead off to end blindly, and others circle to join themselves again. It's tedious. But if you keep going from one to another you'll find a path leading into a road. Following the road you'll finally enter a highway. One cannot travel all the paths, the road and the highway at once. Cutting across fields and woods may cause you to lose your course entirely. Now in this case at hand I have many clues, a number of motives and some suspects. In the end I will have one motive. I'll have one clue of the utmost importance, and the guilty."

"It all sounds beautiful. It seems simple. But *I'm* afraid I'd be going up and down the same road or be traveling in a circle. I'd invariably come back to where I started from. I'd get into a vicious circle."

"You think so, Jack, but experience teaches you to separate chaff from the wheat."

"Well, we'll see in the morning whether you're going to walk into the road or whether you're just on a detour."

"A detour might be an easy way to a solution. That's not a blind road or a circling affair. According to the best authorities that's a long way around."

The conversation went on and on into the night. Finally the soothing effect of the Coon Hollow and a tired feeling caused previous ideas of sleeplessness to dissipate.

"I really think I could sleep now," said Jack. "Two hours ago I thought I never could."

"It wouldn't be a bad idea," yawned Wilbur. "I feel inclined myself. I don't think we'll be molested here. We are four floors above the ground, there's no fire escapes and the doors bolt on the inside."

"Well, sweet dreams," said Jack as he took a "nightcap" and went to the room occupied by Alice.

CHAPTER X

THE RUM RUNNER

THE NIGHT PASSED uneventfully. Early the next morning Wilbur was stirring before either Jack or Alice had awakened. A few hours of sleep refreshed him always even after he had lost nights of rest. He possessed one of those remarkable constitutions that seem to thrive on but little beaming from the son of Somnos. When a peculiar puzzling case engaged his attention he could not sleep beyond a restive period for bodily exertion. And then it seemed his recuperative powers were marvelous. He had hardly arisen when there was a knock upon the door of his room. He went to the door, unlocked it, unbolted it and opened it. Standing before the door was a big broad shouldered man of determined features, coarse in a way. The man wore a plain blue suit and a dark Fedora hat.

"I'm Lieutenant Detective Loomis of the State Department of Safety," said he. "I presume you are Lyman K. Wilbur."

"I am Mr. Wilbur," replied the criminologist as he extended a hand in greeting. "I'm very glad to know you, Mr. Loomis. Come right in."

Mr. Loomis entered and Wilbur rebolted the door. "This is rather an early hour to be calling upon you," the state detective went on. "but whenever I am commissioned by a superior to see anyone at once I do so at the earliest possible moment—if that be in the middle of the night. The Attorney General sent me to you. He told me to assist you in any way that I might. From what little he told me I take it you have a hot case."

"Well, it's not so hot," replied Wilbur as he finished lathering his face preparatory to shaving, a job he had started before Loomis's knock on the door. "It presents more cold trails than a fellow usually runs into on a coon hunt. I've a maze of clues, no accurate deductions and a host of theories."

"Well, if I can't be of any benefit to you other than carrying out the order of my superior I shall be pleased to watch on, if you'll allow me that privilege," said Loomis in reply. "I'd really appreciate it. I've never set the world on fire as a sleuth and I might learn a great deal by watching a great detective work."

"You're flattering, Mr. Loomis," replied Wilbur as he took a stroke at his softened beard with his razor. "I'm really quite an ordinary individual. You are at liberty to accompany me and you may be of great assistance to me. The case is quite out of the ordinary to my way of thinking, and intensely interesting. I believe you are in time to see and participate in some startling revelations. I believe we will see things this morning and be going places. I wired the Governor that I might secure a legal right to open a casket containing the body of a murdered man. He replied that he would secure the necessary authority. It was impossible to secure an autopsy in any other manner. Someone controls every justice of peace in the county."

Continuing his shaving without the use of a mirror, Wilbur stepped to the connecting door of Jack's room and knocked.

"My friend next door is a heavy sleeper," said he.

Jack answered after a prolonged pounding upon the door.

"Get up, you lazy fellow," Wilbur said. "It's time for all good detectives to go to work."

"I'll be with you right away," Jack replied and the thud on the floor was distinct in Wilbur's room as Jack jumped out of bed.

Half an hour later Wilbur, Haughton and Loomis left the Summitville House. It was scarcely six o'clock in the morning. A morning bracer of Coon Hollow called for an immediate breakfast so they sought a restaurant. In Summitville at that hour only one restaurant was functioning. That was an all night affair. As they entered it they noticed that the place was thronged with people. Those within the place were not laborers going to their daily toil, but night hawks who had not yet given themselves up to slumber. Several were maudlin.

"Somebody blew up the cottage next door to Morley's last night," said a tall blonde boy who was waiting on an order of eight hamburgers to go out.

"Yeah, and that's not all," said another who was playing a slot machine and getting lemons with regularity. "The bridge over the Prairie River went up. It damn near sent me to Heaven. Me and the girl friend was hottin' it out to Home Brew Helen's. I just saw the layout in time to stop before playin' Muddy Waters. And don't let nobody tell you them Model A Fords ain't got brakes. I stopped that baby right on the brink of eternity."

"Who done it?" asked the proprietor of the all night food emporium as he patted a raw hamburger into shape.

"That's it," replied the boy at the slot machine who'd punched away five dollars. "No one knows. You could commit a murder in this county and get away with it. All you'd need to do would be to telephone the sheriff about it beforehand so he'd have time enough to be absent. He wouldn't come back until all the tracks were cold."

"Old man Fallows runs the works," ejaculated the proprietor as he hopped a brace of hamburgers over on their back. "Whenever he wants something pulled he tells the sheriff to close his eyes. After the works happens he cautions him again by sayin', 'Don't go too far. You may not run for office next time.' It's a hot town. Per capita this burg has more gangsters than Chicago."

"Where's all the booze comin' from?" asked the blonde boy who was waiting on the sandwiches.

"Santa Claus brings it," replied the owner of the restaurant. "Where do you suppose? This country is dry. What d'you want on the 'burgers—catsup or onion?"

"Onion, you poor sap. Whoever heard of a hamburger without onion," answered the blonde as he lurched and grasped at the counter for support.

Wilbur, Haughton and Loomis sat down at a table. Wilbur called the boy who was rather deeply intoxicated when he started to pick up his bag of sandwiches.

"Beg your pardon, son," said he. "But could you tell me where I might get a little good liquor?"

"You're whoopin' right I can't, mister," returned the blonde. "I'm no stool pigeon."

"Atta boy!" said Jack, and the boy walked back to the counter.

"You fool!" whispered Wilbur disgustedly. "He might have given up some valuable information."

"And if he had you'd never have used the information. I know you. You don't like information you get that way any more than I do," replied Jack.

"Pardon me," said Wilbur. "You're right. Too much Coon Hollow."

"Coon Hollow!" exclaimed the blonde boy who caught the last of Wilbur's remark and returned to the table. "Say, I guess you fellows are regular after all. I'll take you out to the cottage with me so you can get a drink anyhow. It might be a good idea. We've got a party goin' on that looks like it's goin' into another day, an' it's a little shy on men. Albertina Fallows and Lura Tully are out there without their steadies. And believe me there's two Janes that are screams."

"Sure we'll go along," replied Wilbur, whose detective instinct followed the mention of the words Fallows and Tully.

"Well, count me out," said Jack.

"That'll be all right," answered Wilbur. "You go back and get your beauty nap. After a little breakfast we will go out with the boy."

And it so happened that Wilbur and Loomis accompanied the blonde boy to Dory Lake where quite a party was in progress. They arrived at the lake safely in spite of the boy's somewhat uncertain driving and were ushered inside the cottage. Inside was one of those millions of orgies which have been commemorated to Volstead. A radio was blaring forth a hot piece from an orchestra and a few couples were attempting to dance to it. Upon the floor, on lounges, and those niches where dancers were unlikely to trod were those who had "passed out." As it happened, the Fallows and Tully girls were in a fair state of sobriety. The blonde boy introduced Loomis and Wilbur as Mr. Jones and Mr. Smith. Wilbur was very much interested in Albertina Fallows. She was very attractive. In fact the boy had not lied when he had called both girls "screams." Albertina was devastating. She was unaccompanied only because her suitor had been called away from Summitville suddenly. Wilbur perceived that Albertina was sufficiently under the influence of liquor to talk freely. He found her easy to converse with and immediately began to make himself pleasing.

"Would you care to dance, Miss Fallows?" he inquired as the radio flooded the cottage with the strains of another popular dance selection.

"Gladly," she answered. "I've been a little wall flower almost all night."

Wilbur stepped through the dance with Albertina in his arms and reflected as he did so that he wished he was on some other mission in Summitville. She danced divinely and made herself so lovely that he could imagine that he had known her always. While he was so engaged Loomis got along in a very satisfactory manner with Lura Tully.

"That was wonderful," said Albertina when they had finished. "Would you like a little highball? There's some real good stuff in the kitchen. I'm sure I don't care for any of Blondie's hamburgers. Coon Hollow is better, I think. And you know my fiancé says delightfully, 'The food's in the bottle.' That's me all over."

"That's an idea," answered Wilbur. "Let's uncork some."

"Oh boy, it's been uncorked some time. But don't take that or what you see too literally. The unconscious forms that you see were hit with the bar towel. I'm regular myself. And if I do say so, it takes numerous jolts to park me. And I never pass out."

"I admire that. I take my hat off to a girl who can handle the stuff. They're rare."

"Oh, big boy, don't say that. There's quite a few in Summittville that can do it. Give a number of the girls an even start with you and I'll wager they'll be standing up when you're lying down."

"Where is this liquor?" urged Wilbur.

"In the kitchen. Come on." Albertina led the way. In the kitchen two couples were trying to divide a pint four ways.

"Say!" cried Albertina. "What's the big idea? D'you think there's an embargo on? Loosen up!"

"Shush!" said one of the men to the other. "The queen speaks. Divvy up."

The gentleman with the bottle ceased trying to quarter it and gave both Albertina and Wilbur a generous drink.

"Now let's dance again," said Wilbur. "I want to get to know you."

"All right, big boy," replied the girl. "I believe we could get along."

They entered the large living-room of the cottage again and returned to dancing. Loomis and the Tully girl were already on the floor. The two couples were getting along famously and Wilbur was at the point of securing important information from his partner when the door opened suddenly from the outside and a debonair looking gentleman stood revealed. Albertina left Wilbur abruptly and rushing to the doorway threw her arms around the newcomer. Loomis, the Tully girl and two other couples stopped dancing. The man who had just come paid little attention to Albertina's caress. His eyes narrowed perceptibly and his left eyebrow dropped maliciously.

"Why, Bob, what's the matter?" said Albertina aghast. "Don't be jealous. I was just dancing with Mr. Jones. Blondie brought him and Mr. Smith out to the party. Come on and meet them. They're good sports."

"Good sports, eh?" said Bob as he pushed Albertina aside. "They're dicks, both of them."

"Bob!" cried Albertina. "Don't!" She flung herself in front of him as his big right hand suddenly reached for a shoulder holster under his left arm.

"Never mind, Miss Fallows," said Loomis coolly. "Mr. Finlay is covered."

Bob Finlay withdrew his hand from his left armpit for he gazed down a blue steel Police Special. He pushed Albertina away again roughly.

"Good sports?" Finlay snarled. "A couple of snakes! All right, Mr. Loomis, this is the second time we've met. The third time will be the charm!" He turned half savagely to Albertina, "The bird with the gun is a State copper and the other that you've been dancing with is Lyman K. Wilbur, the clever dick that's making a murder out of the Morley case. They've probably pumped you dry."

Albertina Fallows' eyes flashed fire. She flew at Wilbur. "So you're Lyman K. Wilbur? A dick! I wish to God I'd have let him shoot. You—you!"

Wilbur grabbed the hands of the girl as she tried to scratch his eyes out. She was an Amazon when fired. She kicked, struggled, and bit.

"Let me go! Let me go?" she cried furiously in between attempts to bite. "You lice! You dirty coppers!"

"Miss Fallows," Wilbur gently tried to remonstrate.

"Let me go! Let me go!" she cried furiously. "Take your dirty hands off me."

There was a crash behind Wilbur. The gun which Loomis had held leveled at Finlay clattered to the floor. The man who had attempted to split the pint four ways in the kitchen had grabbed a metal candelabrum and knocked the gun from the state detective's hand. Finlay, who had seen the approach from the rear quickly reached for his gun again and withdrew it from the holster.

"Now you dirty bums!" he cried, as he leveled the gun. But the gun never came on a level soon enough to catch Loomis. The detective, a football player of no mean repute in his high school days, tackled Finlay around the feet. The gun went off into the ceiling of the cottage and as Finlay hit the floor Loomis pinioned his gun arm.

Wilbur threw Albertina on an unconscious form upon a couch nearby at the sound of the clattering gun. As Loomis tackled, he dived for the gun of the detective and secured it just before the hands of the candelabrum wielder reached it. He turned quickly on his knees and covered Finlay. Loomis secured Finlay's gun and then quietly slipped a pair of handcuffs on him. While he did this Wilbur turned his attention to the other men, the candelabrum wielder and two others who seemed to sense trouble, if not sufficiently sober to cause any.

"Take them off! Take them off!" cried Albertina Fallows frantically as she dashed to the prostrated Finlay and clawed at his manacles. "You can't do that in my father's cottage. You'll pay for this. I'll have your job, Loomis. My father will get it. You haven't anything on him. You came out here and made all this trouble. Everybody here will swear to it."

"You know we will," said Lura Tully. "It's an outrage."

"You'd better take them off, Loomis," suggested Wilbur. "We really—"

"You bet he'd better take them off," cried Albertina. "And you two better leave or I'll call some real officers."

"Take them off, Loomis," said Wilbur. "We were a little out of place."

"Take them off?" replied Loomis. "Not me! Not when they're on that boy for keeps."

"But we were wrong," Wilbur tried to explain. "We can't hold him."

"Oh, I can't, eh?" replied Loomis as he opened his right hand and revealed a diamond necklace.

"Give me my necklace! That's mine," cried Albertina Fallows.

"You thought it was, Madam," Loomis laughed. "The boy friend gave it to you, no doubt, but I'm afraid he didn't buy it. That necklace is a part of the Westervelt robbery loot. It's a necklace that belonged to Mrs. Westervelt. I saw it fall when you were scuffling with Mr. Wilbur. I noticed it even before that. The peculiar pendant attached to the necklace is the Westervelt Coat of Arms. I don't suppose you or Mr. Finlay even knew it was a Coat of Arms."

"You'll have a sweet time proving your words," said Finlay, who had arisen.

"Oh, I don't know," replied Loomis. "The last occasion of our meeting pretty near linked you with the Westervelt case. You'll have tall explaining to do to show how you came in possession of the necklace. And the theft is nothing. Old man Westervelt was killed cruelly with a sap stick."

"Oh, you're accusing me of murder, eh?" replied Finlay sullenly.

"That's a matter for someone else to decide. Your reputation should hold you instead. I'll admit you've been clever so far. For several years no one has been able to get a thing on you. A jury may acquit you."

"Don't pay any attention to them," said Albertina. "Father will help you out. I'll have him bail you at once."

"I don't believe you can give bail in a charge like this," replied Loomis.

"I'd like to know why."

"It will be murder."

"No! No! It can't be murder."

"All right! Come on, Wilbur," said Loomis. "You'll be wanting to get back to the autopsy. From what I know I don't believe he'll be put in this county jail either."

"I'm very sorry this has all happened, Miss Fallows," Wilbur said consolingly. "I was really not expecting it."

"Oh, yeah!" replied Albertina. "Well, you don't need to apologize. That won't settle this affair. You'll pay for it."

"Well, are we going to get a lift into town or will we have to call a car?" asked Loomis.

"Take my car," said Finlay. "It's been used in Keystone comedies."

"That's thoughtful," returned Loomis. "It looks like a very stunning car. But if it's all the same to you we'll go in Blondie's car. However, I will look your car over." Turning to the boy called Blondie, Loomis asked:

"You'll run us in, won't you?"

"I imagine I'll have to run you in," replied Blondie.

"All right, crank up the flivver," answered Loomis as he grasped Finlay by the arm roughly and pushed him out of the cottage.

Wilbur tried to pacify the Fallows girl further but his effect was all but tragic. A torrent of acrimonious words directed at him was the result. He passed out of the cottage to follow Loomis to the Finlay car. Loomis was inspecting it.

"Swell boat, Mr. Finlay," Loomis said in actual admiration of the car as he tapped the body. "Steel body! Bullet proof glass!" He looked under the car. "And a smoke screen!" he added. "By Jove! You must do a lot of hazardous driving."

"Oh, can the comedy, Loomis," answered Finlay. "Let's get going. You know I'm a bootlegger."

"Oh, I want to look at the interior. It's such an unusual car I must."

Loomis opened the door on the left hand side and inspected the inside.

"Hum!" said he as he inspected the interior carefully. "Ingenious! Light controls from each seat! Well!"

He pressed one of three buttons on the left side in the front seat. There was a report and a bullet ricocheted against the windshield.

"Oh ho!" Loomis continued when he recovered from his surprise and examined the back of the driver's seat. "No wonder you offered your car so magnanimously. I see! You have a revolver set in behind each seat whose firing is electrically controlled. By pushing the right button you can fire from any seat and cause any one of the remaining three to be a death seat. By the driver's seat you have a master control which releases that seat when you enter the car. I take it you always set it when you leave the car. That is very clever—death controlled. When you are driving you can do away with a nocuous occupant very handily and if you happen to be taken for a ride you can do away with the driver or any other occupant. Had we used your car I don't doubt that both

Mr. Wilbur and myself would have proved very nocuous in your presence."

"Let's have a look at that," said Wilbur. "That is interesting."

"Go ahead! Press a button or two, Wilbur," suggested Loomis.

Wilbur did so. He pressed a button on the left side in the rear seat. There was a report and a bullet whizzed from the back seat on the right side.

"Hum! Damn!" said Wilbur in amazement. "I thought all of these clever ingenious things were the province of the big towns. Damn! That is a murder wrinkle. Hum!"

"This boy Finlay is a one o'clock boy in a nine o'clock town," Loomis explained. "He's a big one just caught for the first time. It will probably be the last."

"Say, are you guys going to town?" asked the blond boy whose Ford was barking nearby.

"Sure!" answered Loomis, and turning to Finlay commanded him, "Step lively, big boy."

The blond boy drove carefully into Summittville. He delivered them in front of the Summitville House. Loomis was just debating whether he would go with his prisoner to a neighboring county seat when a roving state police car passed. He hailed it and delivered Finlay into the care of the two officers with instructions to take him on into the state capital for safekeeping.

"That was luck!" said he to Wilbur. "This is my lucky day. I certainly hope it turns out the same for you."

"Did I understand you to say that you expected to learn something from watching me?" countered Wilbur. "From what I've seen I think you can give me some pointers."

"Luck! That's all," smiled Loomis.

The blond boy left his car and edged up to the two detectives.

"Say," said he, "are you two fellows lookin' for a good steer on the Morley case?"

"Right you are, son," answered Wilbur.

"Well, if you'll keep it under your hat I'll give you a crackin' good clue."

Wilbur was not looking for another civilian tip but was willing to chance anything.

"Let's have it. We'll pledge ourselves to secrecy."

"Well, I overheard Bob Finlay talkin' to Fallows a few weeks before the Morley suicide. Morley had just passed them. After he was out of hearin' Finlay said, 'There's a guy that ought to be taken for a ride.' That might have meant something and then again it might not. Anyhow, that's a clue, isn't it? I read crime stories."

"That's a good clue," Wilbur answered the lad. "But it's hearsay."

"Well, the Morley murders might be Finlay's doings," said Loomis as the boy left them. "If they were 'taken for a ride,' Finlay sure had the necessary equipment to do it. Morley might have been linked with him in the bootleg business."

"I don't know," Wilbur answered Loomis truthfully. "It's been my experience that hot trails turn cold and cold trails turn hot. We'll see."

CHAPTER XI

A SURGICAL CASUALTY

WILBUR AND LOOMIS returned to Wilbur's hotel room to pick up Haughton. They briefly recounted their experience at Dory Lake.

"All that I see that you accomplished is the fact that you have another suspect," said Jack after listening. "Of course Loomis has caught Finlay with the goods on him. That's worth while. But the Morley case seems to be just as inexplicable as ever."

"So it seems," replied Wilbur. "But Finlay may talk. We may get a line on Morley's bootlegging business. I'd have questioned him at the Fallows' cottage but I knew it was useless at the moment. He knew I had seen him in Fallows' office too. He won't say anything as long as he relies on Fallows to help him out of his difficulties."

"It's about time for the autopsy, isn't it?" asked Jack.

"It all depends on the prosecutor. I imagine he will use a little haste, though, since the governor and the attorney general have prodded him up. Perhaps we had better go over to LaVell's. Our presence might expedite things."

All three left the hotel and went to the funeral parlors. LaVell admitted them. The expression upon his face showed that he was anything but enthusiastic about their reception, however.

"Meet Detective Lieutenant Loomis of the Department of Safety," said Wilbur. "Mr. Loomis was loaned to us by the State's Attorney's Department."

Loomis grasped LaVell's small effeminate hand in his own huge one and squeezed unmercifully. LaVell winced and his knees sagged.

"I'm glad to meet you, Mr. Loomis," replied LaVell as he withdrew his hand and rubbed it with the other. "What can I do for you gentlemen?"

"The prosecutor will be here directly, and I daresay he intends to hold an autopsy upon both of the Morley bodies. The Attorney General wired me to the effect that he would," said Wilbur.

"Yes, he will be here directly," replied LaVell. "He just called me a short time ago. I don't know who you will get to do Mr. Morley's body, though. That will be terrible."

"Dr. LeClair and Dr. Carter of the State University Medical School will be here by the time the arrangements are completed. I have that information from the Attorney General also. Both are very capable men. Dr. LeClair has been on many cases where I have been in attendance. You have a morgue suitable?"

"Oh yes! You may use my morgue, gentlemen. There's no use in moving the bodies. When Mr. Wilbur was here yesterday I probably acted badly. You must understand one dislikes to have the dead of one's clients disturbed. It's a gruesome experience for relatives and not conducive to good business, even in a certain murder case, much less in an uncertain one. I'll run the bodies down there for your inspection and see that everything is in order. When the prosecutor and the doctors arrive you may come on down. The first door to the right leads into the morgue."

"Thanks, LaVell," replied Wilbur as the undertaker entered another room.

About fifteen minutes later the prosecutor entered. He greeted everyone cordially and amazed Haughton and Wilbur thereby. The difference in his behavior of the night before was pronounced.

"I'm sorry if I've detained you gentlemen," said he. "Have the doctors arrived yet?"

"Not as yet," replied Wilbur.

"I'm very sorry that it was necessary to use such forceful measures to secure these autopsies," said he to Wilbur. "But really I had hardly any other alternative since the county board of supervisors have sat on the cost of things generally. They have ruled that they will authorize the cost of autopsies only in cases where there is a deep suspicion of foul play. Of course when the Attorney General told me to go ahead and have them I could hardly jeopardize my position, even though I feel that both are unjustified. Now that we are going to have them let's hope that we find something of consequence."

"I'll be very much disappointed if we don't find something of interest," replied Wilbur.

"Well, of course that may happen. I took this matter up with a justice of the peace at the county seat and everything is in order for a proper procedure."

"Let's go down to the morgue then," suggested Wilbur. "LaVell took the bodies down there and prepared the place. The doctors will find us."

"Very well."

Wilbur led the way to the morgue, followed by the prosecutor, Loomis and Haughton. They reached it quickly. It was a cold, dank room made out of cement. In the center was a cooling board which sloped from all sides toward the middle. In the midline of it there was a hole where body fluids, blood and other liquids drained into a bucket which sat below the table. The casket containing the remains of Eugene Morley was wheeled close to the cooling board on one side and the one containing the remains of Mrs. Morley was on the other side. Both caskets rested on trucks. Alongside and underneath a window was a sink. Otherwise the room was empty.

Wilbur, after observing these arrangements, raised the windows of the place.

"I imagine fresh air will smell good when the lid comes off that one stiff basket," he remarked as he raised the windows. "If the person inside of that pine is as they say he is we'll want gas masks too."

"Easy Wilbur, easy!" replied Loomis. "My breakfast was light and remember, that Coon Hollow makes for an uplift movement."

"Beg pardon!"

Dr. LeClair and Dr. Carter came into the room.

"This is a hell of a place," said Dr. LeClair. "Isn't there anyone around? I rang the doorbell until I almost developed palsy. Then I walked in. We had the devil's own time finding our way down here."

"The undertaker is busy with his arrangements, I suppose," answered Wilbur as he shook the hands of LeClair and Carter and then introduced them around. "It's a rotten case, fellows. The one corpse was decomposed when found. It went into the box sans embalming, sans anything."

"My kind of a case," answered LeClair. "It just requires goose pimples and guts. Shall we pry the lid?"

"I really think this is a desecrating affair," said the prosecutor. "Don't you think we'd better let them rest in peace? When the lips are silent what good can we possibly do anyhow?"

"The lips may be silent," answered Wilbur who was all but softhearted. "But when the top of that stiff case comes off I'll bet the body is plenty loud."

"Ugh! I thought this affair was on that order. No respect! And the whole affair will turn out a fiasco."

"Oh yeah!" returned Wilbur. "Just like the additional description on that recorded deed. You told the sheriff to bring that over sure, didn't you?"

"He'll be here by the time you've spent the county's money on this useless job."

"Be that as it may, I think what we are about to do is going to help you a great deal in your next campaign."

At this point Wilbur turned to LeClair. "Let's go, doctor," said he.

Doctors LeClair and Carter took off their coats and vests, rolled up their sleeves and slipped into spotless gowns. They deftly donned rubber gloves and Dr. LeClair announced everything was in readiness. Wilbur pried the lid from the hermetically sealed casket.

"Ugh!" exclaimed Loomis as he held his handkerchief over his nostrils.

"It is juicy, isn't it?" laughed Wilbur.

"Give me that spray, Carter," said LeClair.

Dr. Carter handed LeClair the spray, and the doctor vigorously applied the deodorizer.

"That bird is certainly dead," said LeClair as he sprayed. "There's no doubt of that. What I get is not the breath of life."

With the spraying the terrible odor lessened somewhat. Doctors LeClair and Carter took a look at the corpse along with Wilbur.

"Hum! They never took his underwear off," said LeClair.

"And there's lye in the coffin," observed Dr. Carter.

"Lye!" exclaimed the prosecutor.

"Sure there's lye in it," said Wilbur. "What did you expect the undertaker would use? Alcohol?"

"I—I didn't expect—"

"That's all right," answered Wilbur, as his eye caught a sudden widening of the prosecutor's eyes at the mention of alcohol. "Alcohol is used sometimes to preserve specimens. Lye, however, destroys them."

"Of course I was just asking for information."

"And of course I was just informing you," Wilbur replied curtly.

"Let's get him out of the casket and upon the cooling board," said LeClair.

"All right, let's do," replied Wilbur.

"Where's the undertaker? He ought to know how to get a decomposed corpse out of a casket. We can take it out all right but he ought to know an easy way."

"That's right, he should," replied Wilbur. "He knew how to get one in and continue the decomposition." Turning to Loomis Wilbur said, "Go get LaVell, Loomis."

Loomis went to do Wilbur's bidding. He was very glad to get out of the morgue a few moments. He was gone some time and then returned.

"There isn't a soul in this house," said he. "I've searched from top to bottom, yelled till I'm almost hoarse and there's no one answered me, and I saw no one."

"Maybe he just stepped out for the moment," suggested the prosecutor. "He might have received a call."

"He received a call all right," answered Wilbur. "It was urgent. And if you ask me he'll be gone for more than a moment. I really don't believe he'll come back until someone goes after him."

The prosecutor turned red and went to the window. "That stench is terrible," said he.

"Which one?" asked Wilbur. The prosecutor did not reply to Wilbur's remark.

"Well, let's get it out," said LeClair. "The skin may slip and the flesh cleave from the bone but it's got to be done."

"Let's turn the casket upside down over the board," suggested Carter.

"Good idea!" said LeClair.

They all took hold of the casket, lifted it above the cooling board and rolled the body out gently. Dr. LeClair sprayed the body furiously.

The body of Eugene Morey was beyond any recognition. Time, decomposition and lye had got in their work. It might be hard to prove a suicide or a murder. While Dr. LeClair prepared to probe the two bullet wounds, Wilbur examined them. When Dr. Le Clair returned to the body with his instruments Wilbur spoke.

"Doctor," said he, "I crave the privilege of extracting a couple of grains of powder that I see clinging to the entrance of that head wound."

"Go ahead, old man. Certainly!" answered LeClair. "I saw them. That is black powder. What of it?"

"They're not grains of Ballistite powder?" asked Wilbur.

"Oh, my no! There's too many powder marks. You'd have to hunt for it if that were Ballistite powder."

"I knew that, doctor. I just wanted your corroboration," replied Wilbur as he picked a few grains from the temple of the corpse. Securing his precious grains of powder Wilbur continued, "Go ahead, doctor."

The doctor ran a probe into the track caused by the bullet. His probe came out at the other side of the head.

"Through and through," said he. "No bullet to be retrieved there. That's too bad, for as I understand it you have the gun."

"Too many guns," answered Wilbur.

"Oh!" answered LeClair. "Well, let's hope there's one in the heart region."

The probing in the heart region revealed a through and through wound also.

"That's too bad. Honestly that's maddening," said LeClair. "There's no chance of ever finding those bullets, I suppose."

"No matter, doctor," replied Wilbur. "I've got the powder. I think that will be sufficient. Proceed with the autopsy."

Dr. LeClair secured his scalpels, rib-cutting shears and necessary instruments to do a complete post mortem.

"Here goes," said he. "My sense of smell is gone. How's yours, Carter?"

"I don't smell anything," replied Carter.

"Liars," said Loomis. Both doctors laughed.

"Let's cut the underwear off, Carter, and do a thorough job," said LeClair as he took a pair of shears and cut the underwear from the corpse. In the midline of the body above the umbilicus was the healed scar of an abdominal operation.

"Did Morley have an abdominal operation at any time?" asked LeClair.

"Yes, so they say," answered Wilbur as he too noted the scar barely discernible on account of the decomposition.

"Well offhand I'd say this operation was recent but one cannot tell on account of the putrefaction," returned LeClair. "Anything you want to look at, Wilbur, before we mutilate these beautiful remains?"

"Nothing! Post him!"

"Here goes," said LeClair as he cut a long gash from Morley's neck to the symphasis pubes. It required little effort. He inspected the interior of the abdomen.

"This belly is full of pus!" exclaimed LeClair as he strained to look into the interior of Morley along with Carter.

"This bird had a violent peritonitis when he died. You don't suppose he did commit suicide to end his suffering?"

"Hum! Damn!" exclaimed Wilbur as he looked at Haughton while his face went crimson. The prosecutor grinned. Loomis had turned away and was breathing heavily at the window.

"What caused it?" asked Wilbur.

"In a minute I'll tell you," said LeClair as he fished around in the belly. After a few moments he exclaimed, "It's been a gastro-intestinal thing! Things don't feel right about the stomach." He continued to feel about and then suddenly snorted. "I've got it! It's been a gastroenterostomy. And someone's done it with the old oblong button. That's Murphy's old trick! Someone who learned surgery under John B. Murphy or someone who took to his button did this work."

"Well, I'll be damned!" exclaimed Wilbur. "It can't be, that's all."

"Well, here it is," said LeClair, as he brought the stomach and jejunum out of the abdomen. He made a clear cut into the stomach and extracted the Murphy button.

"God, doctor, this is terrible!" exclaimed Wilbur who was all confusion. "This man had that operation and a peritonitis. There was a reason, then, for his committing suicide. Still he must have been murdered."

Carter and LeClair looked at Wilbur in amazement. Jack's jaw dropped. The prosecutor smiled as he lit a cigarette.

"Why does it particularly have to be murder?" asked LeClair.

"Well those powder marks were those of black powder, weren't they?"

"Most assuredly."

"Well the gun Morley is supposed to have killed himself with was loaded with shells that had Ballistite powder in them."

"What?" asked LeClair and Carter in unison.

"Absolutely."

"Then the two cartridges fired were charged with black powder and were mixed up with some that were loaded with Ballistite," replied LeClair. "That's possible. Or else the gun was minus two cartridges when Morley picked it up and he simply put two black powder shells in to fill out."

"It might be," returned Wilbur who hated to admit defeat. "But why would a man committing suicide need full chambers when he had enough cartridges to do the deed?"

"Hum! I don't know," answered LeClair. 'The gun might have been loaded that way long before he contemplated suicide."

"Go ahead. I'm beat for the moment at least."

"Doctor, may I ask a question?" said the prosecutor.

"Surely," returned LeClair.

"Is it customary for a surgeon to leave those buttons in a person?"

"Oh, that's nothing," replied LeClair. "Sometimes a surgeon is a little careless. I've known cases where they lost hemostats, sponges, scissors, and God only knows what in an open belly."

"Oh!" exclaimed the prosecutor. "No operations for me."

"God, but you birds are callous," said Loomis.

"I was just having a little fun, prosecutor," said LeClair. "These buttons are supposed to pass on out of the bowels after they serve the purpose of joining a new stomach opening to a new opening in the bowel."

"Well now," Wilbur broke in again after some deep thinking. "Since that button did not pass, that operation must have been recent."

"Most likely," returned LeClair.

"Did Morley ever have any stomach trouble?"

"I've heard him complain," said the prosecutor.

"You would," snapped Wilbur.

"Well, I'm the only one here who would know. Maybe Morley went away to undergo an operation, half way recovered and because the button did not pass developed a peritonitis. Wouldn't it be natural to suppose that he ended his misery with a bullet? I'd imagine he was in terrible pain."

"Undoubtedly," put in LeClair.

"I don't believe that a man who had undergone such an operation could get back to his cottage with a peritonitis, much less want to do so when he knew the button was still in him. His surgeon wouldn't permit him to do it."

"You would!" exclaimed the prosecutor dryly. "I hope you are able to prove the falsification of the record of that deed with as much ability as you have demonstrated the murder."

"Nuts!" answered Wilbur. "I'm not done with this case. I've a thirty-two caliber gun in my possession which was found near Bakers Landing. It was fired twice and the cartridges in it were loaded with black powder."

"Oh yeah!" answered the prosecutor. "Well, I've got a gun over at my house that hasn't been fired since the Civil War."

"Bah!" snarled Wilbur.

"Should I proceed any further, Mr. Wilbur?" asked Le-Clair.

"There's nothing to be gained," answered the criminologist in a crestfallen manner. "Sew him up."

"Sew that body up?" questioned LeClair. "I'd like to see someone do it. The stitches wouldn't hold. Hold the casket and I'll tumble him back in." Wilbur, Loomis, Carter and the prosecutor held the casket to the edge of the cooling board. LeClair rolled the remains back into the casket.

CHAPTER XII

POISON!

"LET'S GO TAKE A SMOKE," suggested LeClair, "before we begin on the other body. Or do you desire it posted now, Wilbur?"

"I certainly want the other body posted," answered the criminologist. "I'm not going to give up until I've exhausted every means at my disposal."

"Well, I'm here to serve you after I have a smoke. The worst one is behind me. The lady should not be out of the ordinary."

"I think this affair is ridiculous," put in the prosecutor. "I can't see any sane reason for mutilating that poor woman's remains. An autopsy of her body will probably reveal less than the autopsy of her husband did. It's simply terrible."

"Oh, there's nothing so terrible about it," said LeClair. "And both of them ought to settle this dispute once and for all."

"You don't feel like a layman," replied the prosecutor. "You're hardened. I'd hate to see members of my family hacked up after death."

"It's legal. It's the only thing to do," put in Carter. "After all, a body is a body. We're not hurting the soul."

"Oh, very well!" replied the prosecutor. "Go ahead. You can't get my viewpoint and I can't get yours. You have the authority to proceed. But it does seem terrible to me that an outsider can come in here and stir such a thing up when our officers had already deduced the causes of the deaths. They may not be as smart as some city people but they get along."

Loomis and Haughton had nothing to say. Both of them were sorry for Wilbur. It looked as if his investigation was a complete failure. They accompanied the rest outside in silence and joined in the smoking.

"I can see that you're terribly disappointed, Wilbur," said LeClair, as he inhaled deeply of a cigarette. "It's really too bad that we did not recover at least one of the bullets."

"A thirty-two caliber bullet that had been fired from a Smith and Wesson revolver would have definitely set the case down as one of murder," replied Wilbur. "But a thirty-two caliber bullet that had been fired from a Colt would have proved nothing. I had hoped to find the former so I'm disappointed naturally. The thing that knocks the props from under me is the peritonitis, and that Murphy button. How long might a button remain in a person?"

"I really couldn't say. If you will consult any standard text book on surgery you might learn."

"I don't believe the evidence. How would a man get to a cottage on Ramona Lake as ill as Morley without help? Would anyone bring him there in such a condition and leave him? If someone did bring him there why are they silent?"

"There's the wife."

"And the uncle, of course! I haven't interviewed him at all. It was my intention to do that after the autopsy. And where has LaVell gone? Why did he go?"

"I don't know, Wilbur. You're the detective," answered LeClair. "I'm only a doctor. All I know about the case is this: the findings of the autopsy do not point to murder. If murder has been done it is lamentable that no proofs have been left behind."

"You're quite right. A murder theory is out of order at present. Well, let's drop the Eugene Morley case and investigate the death of Mrs. Morley. Are you ready?"

"Quite."

Returning to the morgue, the body of Mrs. Morley was taken out of the casket and the doctors proceeded to post it. The procedure was the same as in the case of the husband except for the fact that the entire viscera were taken from the body before any examination other than cursory was made. There was nothing to point to the direct seat of trouble as in the case of the husband. The usual tabulation of external appearances was taken down by Carter before the incision. After the excision of the viscera LeClair opened the stomach.

"Liquor in the stomach," LeClair pronounced at once. "Well defined odor."

"That's something," murmured Wilbur in the faint hope that at least one of his suppositions would survive. "Anything else?"

"Yes," answered LeClair. "The stomach is red and inflamed as from an irritant poison."

"Aha!" ejaculated Wilbur.

LeClair poured the stomach contents into one of a number of sterilized jars and then examined the mucosa of the stomach.

"Have you a glass, Wilbur?" he asked.

"Right here," answered Wilbur as he pulled his magnifying glass, which he always carried, from a pocket.

LeClair ran over the stomach with the glass. "Offhand I would say it was a case of arsenical poisoning. There is something that appears to be actual arsenic in the stomach. However that's up to the toxicologist."

"You are certain, however, of an irritant poison?" said Wilbur.

"Well, I've done about three thousand post mortems and I've found arsenic in bodies enough times to make me feel certain of my ground."

"She must have committed suicide," said the prosecutor.

"Or she was murdered," interjected Wilbur.

"Oh piffle!" snapped the public officer. "You'd have everybody murdered."

"I can't settle the argument, gentlemen," LeClair smiled. "But you may be sure of one thing, she either committed suicide or was murdered."

"Well, how are you going to prove which it was?" asked the prosecutor.

"From the autopsy that is impossible," replied LeClair.

"Hum! Then this affair turned out just as I said it would. You've done the autopsies and don't know any more than before you did them. It's poppycock! Piffle! I guess the commissioners were right. All I see that's been accomplished is the fact that the county owes another bill."

"No, I think we know more than we did," replied LeClair. "And we're at least positive about what we do know. We know that Morley had a peritonitis and a Murphy button in him besides two bullet holes. We know that Mrs. Morley was killed by an irritant poison."

"In other words—they're dead," laughed the prosecutor insipidly.

"Murdered," said Wilbur almost viciously.

"Ha! Ha! Ha!" laughed Wilbur's nemesis. "Tell me another of your famous exploits some other time. Well, I must be going. I do hope that everyone is satisfied however. I'm very glad to have made the acquaintance of all of you. It's been a charming morning. Good-by!"

"Never mind, Wilbur," said Haughton, after the prosecutor was gone. "It isn't your fault. I shouldn't have called you on such a lousy case."

"It isn't a lousy case, Jack," Wilbur replied. "It's a great case. I'm not through. Not by a jugful."

"I certainly admire your visceral fortitude, Mr. Wilbur," put in Loomis. "You're a sticker."

"Sure I'm a sticker. I see what you see. It looks like there was no way under the heavens to make a murder charge stick. It fact it looks like there wasn't one murder, much less two."

"It sure does," said Loomis.

"Maybe so. If there hasn't been foul play why are so many people evasive? Why have some people attempted Haughton's life, his wife's and mine? Why did they not want to have an autopsy?"

"The liquor racket, Lyman," suggested Jack. "Just as we figured. That might all have been the doings of your friend Finlay."

"I don't think so."

"He's a stubborn cuss. Give him credit," laughed LeClair as he and Carter bottled up the remainder of the organs essential to a toxicological examination.

"Well, hurry up fellows," said Wilbur with a forced smile. "Let's get going."

"We'll be right with you," replied LeClair. The doctors finished their work, donned their street clothes and the entire assemblage left the morgue. In the funeral parlor office the sheriff and the prosecutor awaited them.

CHAPTER XIII

BLACK LIGHT

"I'VE BEEN WAITING for you to appear, Mr. Wilbur," said the sheriff when they had all entered the office. "I brought the record of that deed over as you suggested. The prosecutor has just been telling me about the results of the autopsies. I've also got a warrant for the arrest of your friend Mr. Haughton. It's not serious, understand. Just possession of intoxicating liquors. I just couldn't do no different finding that liquor on his premises. You understand. It's only a year and a thousand dollar fine."

"Why you damned infernal fool!" yelled Jack. "That's good!"

"I'll say it is," replied the sheriff. "Plenty of evidence and found on your property unless your great detective friend Wilbur can Houdini you out of your own signature."

"Gentlemen," said Wilbur to Loomis and the two doctors, "This is another of the many unexplainable happenings which cause me to believe the Morley deaths have something to do with a gigantic plot. Mr. Haughton's deed to his Ramona Lake property burned up in his cottage. He purchased the cottage of Morley. Morley and his wife are dead. Morley's cottage, the murder cottage, and its grounds joined Mr. Haughton's land. Since liquor was found in Morley's cottage, a description of that cottage and its grounds has been added to the original description of Haughton's cottage and ground. I'm going to prove that it was added. I'd like to have all of you accompany me to a doctor's office."

"Doctor's office!" exclaimed the sheriff. "What's a doctor's office got to do with it?"

"Never mind, Mr. Sheriff! This is my trick."

"Let him go," said the prosecutor. "It'll just be another autopsy."

The entire party proceeded to Doctor Shaw's office, the place where Alice had received attention for the injury to her arm. Dr. Shaw was in.

"This is sort of an imposition, Doctor," said Wilbur after he had introduced everyone to the doctor. "But I noticed you had an ultra-violet lamp when you gave Mrs. Haughton attention. I would like very much to use the lamp and will pay you well for the same."

"Tut! Tut!" replied Dr. Shaw. "Go ahead and use the lamp."

"Go back to the hotel, Jack," said Wilbur at this point, "and bring my alligator grip."

Jack did as directed and soon returned with the grip from which Wilbur took a set of ultra-violet light filters.

"This is a set of ultra-violet filters made by the Corning Glass Works," said Wilbur as he took the same from his grip. "As you all probably do not know, and a million of others, a filter glass has been perfected which permits the passage of invisible ultra-violet or black light, and prevents the passage of the luminous rays from the source of the ultraviolet. Wood's nickel oxide filter glass was the first of these filters which permitted examination of excited luminescence aroused only while objects are under the influence of the activating light. This is known as fluorescence or phosphorescence as you choose, since there is only a slight mark of difference in the two phenomena."

"Show us your trick," said the sheriff, whose education was a thing that had been garnered from a barn lot.

"All right," replied Wilbur. "Has anyone false teeth?"

"I have," said the sheriff.

"Step in the light," replied the criminologist who now had the ultra-violet lamp in operation and the filter functioning.

The sheriff did as directed.

"You will notice the sheriff's false teeth are a chocolate color under black light. Now someone with natural teeth take the sheriff's place."

Haughton stepped forward.

"Notice the difference," said Wilbur. "Mr. Haughton's teeth fluoresce a brilliant white." Haughton stepped out of the light.

"The finger nails fluoresce vividly under black light. And, gentlemen, if a person has had a manicure and the nails polished it is possible to estimate when they were polished because of the difference in the fluorescence of the polish and the fluorescence of the natural nail. The growth of a nail is about one thirty-second of an inch a week."

"All right! All right!" said the sheriff as he handed the record of the Haughton deed to Wilbur. "We're not interested in teeth and fingernails. Show us where this record has been altered."

"Gladly," replied Wilbur as he took the record and put it under the black light.

The result was astounding. There was an evident difference in the description of Haughton's property and that of Morley's.

"There you are, gentlemen," said Wilbur coolly. "The two descriptions were put on that record at different times. Not only that but the ink was different in each case. The description of Morley's property was put on that record recently. The description of Haughton's sometime before."

"Certainly, anybody can see that," said Loomis.

"Even I see it," said the prosecutor and for him it was quite an admission.

"Well, I'll be damned," said the sheriff. "That's pretty cute."

Doctor LeClair and Doctor Carter only laughed. The phenomenon was not new to them.

"Black light will detect the man who alters his books," replied Wilbur. "It will reveal the so-called invisible writing without changing the paper or material it is written upon. It will detect spurious paintings, diamonds and pearls. It has been used extensively to read the ancient sheepskin writings of monks. The more recent monks decided what was written upon the old sheepskins was worth nothing and they wrote over the original faded writing. Now today when we are in search of ancient ideas the old writings are of value. These sheepskins examined under black light reveal the older writings. That in a measure is what we see in this deed record."

Wilbur turned to the sheriff and continued, "Now if you want to serve your warrant upon my friend Mr. Haughton go ahead and do so."

"I'm going to tear it up," answered the sheriff. "There's no use pushing a case when you're beaten at the start. But I'd like to find out who altered that record."

"That might not be hard to do," answered Wilbur. "Suppose you try."

"I'll do that, Mr. Wilbur. Just keep this little matter quiet. I'll do a little nosing around."

"Be careful that you don't bite the hand that's feeding you," Wilbur shot hastily.

"I think we'd better be going, Sheriff," said the prosecutor.

"I'm sorry you can't stay and see some other marvelous uses of black light. It's really wonderful. It's one of the many new scientific methods to detect crime. There are many others. The criminal today has a poor chance. He is dumb when pitted against science. It's really pathetic when one stops to consider—he is caught before he starts his crime, thanks to science. And, my dear friends, although the Morley deaths seem to have passed as suicides I am afraid that they will be revealed as murders in the end, just as I have demonstrated that there was an addition to the record of the deed."

"Gentlemen, we really must be going," said the sheriff.

"Very sorry," replied Wilbur. "I'm terribly sorry. But we'll be seeing you."

There was an implication in Wilbur's last remark that the sheriff and the prosecutor did not fail to get. They left, however, and not without chagrin.

"Thanks, Dr. Shaw, for the use of the lamp, if that repays you," said Wilbur as he placed the filters back in his grip.

"Don't mention it at all," returned the doctor. "I'm glad to have aided you. Where could I secure one of those filters?"

"The Corning Glass Works."

"Thanks. I'd like to experiment myself. That's the reason of my question."

"Well, men," said Wilbur as he put the filters away, "let's repair to the Summitville House. Haughton has some rare Coon Hollow over there and I really think he ought to buy the rounds after I've helped him out of that jam."

"The suggestion isn't half bad," replied LeClair.

"I imagined you could stand a portion, doctor," winked Wilbur. "You should need a stomachic after your morning's work."

"I think I'll be going," said Loomis.

"Oh no, don't do that," importuned Wilbur. "Just because you're a state detective! We'll say nothing. And don't think you're the only state or national officer that's imbibing the forbidden stuff. They're at it from the senate down."

"I'd run over myself if I had the time," put in Doctor Shaw.

"Do that, doctor!" encouraged Haughton.

"Well—sure I will."

"It's a great institution—the Eighteenth Amendment," Wilbur laughed.

CHAPTER XIV

THE LADY TAKES A HAND

EVERYONE ENJOYED his highball just as most everyone does anything which is obtained through a little lawlessness. The average mind is thrilled at the thought of forbidden fruit. In fact, the makeup of man seeks a thrill. It is lawless to steal a watermelon from a farmer's patch, yet who is there that denies the pleasure of a melon obtained in that manner? Stolen sweets are sweetest. Hence the failure of prohibition. Alice, a past master of mixing any and all kinds of alcoholic concoctions, did the serving after an introduction by Wilbur.

"That's ripping," was LeClair's comment.

"None better since I left Le Havre," said Carter.

"Good Canadian," observed Loomis whose contact with the Canadian border qualified him as an expert.

"It's Coon Hollow, isn't it?" asked Dr. Shaw as he inspected the bottle, and then added, "I thought so. It's about the only bonded we get around here."

"It isn't bad," remarked Wilbur. "I'm interested in it. I'd like to know how it happens to be here in quantity. Not that I want to put anybody in the toils for furnishing it! Far be it! Personally, I regard it as a business—an extremely hazardous one. But I would like to know about the particular traffic in this region because I think it would throw some light upon the Morley deaths."

"You have a very strange case," said LeClair. "I'll be interested in following it. And if a murder has been done I wish you all the success possible. I can see where the liquor traffic might enter into it."

"Well, gentlemen, I'm sorry I cannot remain with you longer," said Loomis. "I'm pleased to have met you all and hope to have the pleasure of seeing you again." Turning to Wilbur he addressed him directly, "There's nothing further that I can do for you, is there?"

"Oh yes, Loomis," replied Wilbur. "I want you to do two things. First, I want you to question Finlay closely about his connection with Morley and Fallows. Try and wring something out of him. I doubt if you'll get much. But try. Secondly, I want you to take up the chase of Pierre LaVell."

"I'd better start on LaVell at once then."

"If you will please. I can't see my way clear at the present."

"Very well! I'll try and get some trace of him in town before I leave. After that I'll report in at headquarters and question Finlay. Then I'll put all of my energies on LaVell. You think he's gone?"

"I know he's gone. The quicklime in that coffin tells me that. It wasn't put there to destroy the odor of that corpse as a few people imagine. There was some other reason. LaVell has flown."

"Well, the quicker I get busy then the better."

"Right you are," replied Wilbur, as he grasped the detective's hand. "Glad to have met you; glad you captured Finlay and hope you get a promotion,"

"I'm not caring for the promotion. There's a ten thousand dollar reward for the apprehension of the killer of old man Westervelt. I'm hoping I get that."

"I'm betting on you."

"Well, you'll hear from me the minute I get any definite trace of LaVell."

"I must be going too," said Doctor Shaw. "It's my dinner time."

"Yes, and we'll be going—Dr. LeClair and myself," said Carter.

"Just one more?" suggested Wilbur.

"No thanks," replied Carter.

"There's no use working a good horse to death," said LeClair.

"One's enough for me," Dr. Shaw said, with upraised hands. "My patients will all smell this one on my breath."

And so Haughton, Wilbur and Alice were left alone.

"Well, tell me about it," said Alice when the guests had departed. "What is it all about?"

Briefly Wilbur told of everything that had transpired.

"I've never in all my experience bumped into such a mess," said he when he finished. "Where is the money? Where is LaVell? Were the Morleys murdered or did each one commit suicide? What were the motives activating either the murders or the suicides? Why are we all so obnoxious if there is nothing wrong? Who deliberately left a glove like yours upon the lake beach and wears shoes off as you do? Are there two persons with those identical characteristics? Why were Morley's clothes burned up? What of the two guns, even though the difference in the powder can be explained? Why are the numbers filed off the gun loaded with the black powder shells? If there have been two murders executed they are almost, if not quite, perfect crimes. I don't know what to do or which way to turn. It does seem, though, that there must be a key to the mystery."

"The alteration of that record gets me," said Jack. "That's a bold piece of work—and the object?"

"Ostensibly it was done to harass us," Wilbur explained. "But for an examination under black light you would be the owner of the Morley cottage."

"But it's preposterous," returned Alice.

"Yes, we know it is but the examination under black light is the only way we could prove it to others. But for that, Jack would have been railroaded. However, I don't think the liquor idea was the main reason for the attempt to show Jack as the owner. That was but the beginning of a plot. With you proven as the owners of the cottage it would have been very easy to throw the suspicion of being the murderers of the Morleys upon you."

"It would have!" exclaimed Alice with a look of horror. "The dastardly demons!"

"This thing is clever. It's been hatched in a master mind," Wilbur went on. "The thing has been cleverly thought out beforehand. All of the intricacies were methodically planned. What is false? The false seems true and the true appears false. It behooves us to weigh every move we make. There are pitfalls all about us. Now, getting back to the record alterations, or additions, to be more correct; if the idea was to throw the suspicion of murder upon us and I say us because I would have come in for my share, then we must have unearthed something which the real murderers consider more than warm. There must have been a murder or murders committed, using that theory as a premise. Now what have we discovered that points to the murder theory the strongest?"

"I don't know," answered Jack.

"And who knew that we had obtained this information?" Wilbur continued. "It wasn't the slippers or the gloves because we told no one of them. It wasn't the finding of the Smith and Wesson either, because no one knew of that until today. Was it the shank buttons with the blue serge covering? Was it the whiskey cache and the underground tunnel?"

"I think it was the discovery of the buttons," said Alice. "I can't see where the liquor and tunnel would point toward a murder directly, that is, to arouse a deep suspicion that we knew there had been a murder. The buttons would—the proof of a desire to conceal something."

"And that takes us to LaVell. His disappearance points the finger of guilt at him all the more. And why did he object to the post mortems so strenuously when we actually found so little? If he were behind this whole affair and knew that the autopsies could reveal no more than they did, why did he object? Why did he disappear? It's hard for me to believe a man could be so astute to plan a flawless affair and not remain to see it through."

"He's not alone," said Jack.

Alice studied hard.

"No, he's not alone in it," replied Wilbur. "But everything points to the fact that he was the most active."

"The refusal of every officer in this county to order an autopsy proves there were plenty in it."

"It seems to indicate that Fallows was on the 'in,' at least."

"It's a mess. You named it right."

"Well, let's get dinner. I'm about starved," suggested Wilbur. "After dinner I'm going to do a little shoe investigating. I can't get away from footprints; the mysterious glove that mates those of your wife, and the shank buttons."

"Dinner sounds awfully good to me," said Alice. "You know I didn't have any breakfast."

"So you didn't, honey," answered Jack. "We'll go at once."

"And after dinner I'm going to do a little sleuthing," remarked Alice.

"Good! Great! What's the idea?" asked Wilbur.

"Never you mind," replied Alice. "It's just an idea."

CHAPTER XV

A SEARCH FOR A SURGEON

AFTER APPEASING his gastronomic want, Wilbur decided to begin a process of elimination as he had done many times before on cases which stumped him. Accordingly he bade Jack and Alice good-by with the understanding that they would meet later at the hotel. Leaving them, he went directly to Smith's big shoe store.

Mr. Smith, the proprietor of the store, greeted him cordially as Wilbur made known his name and business.

"I am wondering if you might recall any of your customers who wear their shoes off in this manner," said Wilbur as he produced a pair of Alice's shoes which he had stuck in his pocket. "It's just a mere chance that you would."

"Let me think. That's rather a large order and I don't believe I can fill it," said Mr. Smith as he examined the shoes. "I rarely if ever take any notice of just how shoes are worn down. You know most everyone wears his shoe soles and heels off to some extent. I'll confess, though, that this case is singular."

Mr. Smith thought for some time in silence. "I can only think of two women whose shoes I have ever noticed in this particular connection," Mr. Smith finally said. "And then I cannot say whether either one of them wore the heel and sole off as they are worn off in these shoes. I have simply noted the fact that they wore heels off in some manner—just a casual observance."

"I understand. I didn't expect you to give me any definite information."

"Well, Mrs. Morley wore her shoes off at the heels and soles constantly."

"Is that so? That's illuminating."

"The other lady is totally unconnected with the case you are unraveling, I am sure—Albertina Fallows, the daughter of Ambrose Fallows, the attorney."

"There are no others whom you recall?"

"Oh, there are lots of women, of course, but these two are the only ones I recall where I have any vivid remembrance—extreme cases. I would imagine you could gain more substantial information at a cobbler's. Women might have shoes which they liked well, repaired."

"I was intending to do that. Where is most of the repair work done?"

"Herman, the cobbler, has a place in the next block. I send all of my repair work to him. He does about all the repair work that is done in the city."

"I thank you very much for the information you have given me and assure you that it will go no further," said Wilbur as he left. "I'll call upon the cobbler."

"Damn!" Wilbur exclaimed when he was outside the shoe store. "The breaks in this case are rotten. I wonder if Mrs. Morley made those tracks. Damn it all! And Albertina Fallows! She may have made the prints. She might have been with Bob Finlay. Well, we'll see."

From Smith's shoe store Wilbur went to the shop of Herman, the cobbler. Always with an eye for business, Herman arose from his bench and came shuffling forward when he saw Wilbur enter with the shoes under his arm.

"Yes, vot can I do for you?" asked Herman.

"I was wondering if you remember repairing a pair of shoes like these at any time. Do you do work for any lady who runs off a heel of one shoe and the sole of another?" asked Wilbur as he demonstrated the condition of the shoes.

"Hum! Let me think," answered Herman as he scratched his head. After a moment he raised his right hand in confirmation of an idea and turned to his bench. "Uh huh, I think I do. I tink I got a pair like them in for repair."

"I'll be very glad to see them," said Wilbur.

"I noticed them because it is seldom dat a voman vears her shoes off dat vay and vot is more de late generation very seldom bodders mit repairin'. Dey usually trow de worn shoes away and buy a new pair. De shoe repairing business isn't so good as it used to be in the nineties."

Herman rummaged in his collection of shoes which had been brought in for repair. Wilbur waited anxiously.

"Hum! De shoes are gone," said Herman when he had gone through the pile. "Dey vere here. And I know dat I did not repair dem."

"Go through them again please," said Wilbur. "Maybe you overlooked them."

Herman again went through his pile of shoes. "No, dey are not here," said he blankly as he scratched his head.

"Whose shoes were they?"

"De name was on de shoes. I don't remember but a lady brought dem in dat's living in a cottage on Ramona Lake."

"A Mrs. Haughton?" Wilbur suggested.

"Dat's it. A Mrs. Haughton."

"Now they're gone and you're sure she did not get them?"

"Oh no, she didn't get dem. She brought dem in sometime ago and said dere vas no hurry."

"Good!" exclaimed Wilbur.

"Not so good," replied Herman. "Suppose de lady comes for de shoes?"

"She won't, Herman. I'll see to that," replied Wilbur. "And don't let this little call disturb you. I am a criminologist investigating the Morley deaths. What you have told me goes no further."

"Oh, the Morleys! They were my best customers. They were so saving. I repaired many shoes for both Mr. and Mrs. Morley. I do hope you find the murderers, if murder has been done."

"I'll do what I can," replied Wilbur.

Wilbur started out of the shop and then stopped short. "Oh, by the way," said he to the cobbler. "You don't think you could have given Mrs. Morley that pair of shoes by mistake?"

"Oh my no! The shoes were not repaired."

"That's right. Hum!"

Wilbur stepped out of the cobbler's shop. A woman passed as he did so. She was strangely familiar. As Wilbur's eyes followed her figure they came to rest upon her shoes. Albertina Fallows! He followed her. He noted the heel of one shoe was run over slightly. He hastily looked at those in his hand. "Right!" he exclaimed to himself. Passing over to the left of the woman he noticed that the left foot seemed to scrape the sole as she walked. The shoes were relatively new and of course would show but little wear. Albertina Fallows entered the building which housed her father's office.

"I'm mad! I'm crazy!" Wilbur said to himself. "All the women in the world don't wear their shoes off alike. I'm batty! It just shows how a detective's mind gets, in time. Here I am running around pursuing women's shoes and already I have the same kind on Albertina Fallows, Mrs. Haughton, Mrs. Morley and someone else. I'd scream right now if I saw another woman's glove with a padded little finger. I'll have to get somewhere on this case soon or I'll be a walking delegate for the booby hatch. Then there's the missing pair from Herman's shop. Who's wearing them? Oh God! I'm following everything and nothing. I'm just plain goofy. It's a good thing the Bankers' Indemnity don't know that I'm chasing enough ladies' shoes to start a store with or I'd be fired."

Wilbur lit a cigarette. While searching for a match he felt the shank coat buttons in his pocket.

"And coat buttons!" he exclaimed. "That's probably another goofy idea. No wonder I got the laugh at the autopsies. It begins to look as if I'm a downright ass—trying to make two murder cases with clues of shoe soles and coat buttons when in reality the cases prove to be suicides. I'm more than buggy."

And so Wilbur ruminated on his way back to the hotel. It looked like a mess only explainable on a suicide hypothesis.

If the Morley deaths were murders it looked as if they were perfect crimes. Everything was a conjecture. The dynamited bridge, the exploded cottage and the peculiar construction of the Morley cottage were not even explained. The causes, the whys and the wherefores, were only guesses. What little was known definitely, as the autopsy results, were at variance with what was suspected. It was no wonder that Wilbur was in an agitated mood when he met Jack and Alice at the hotel.

"Suicides my eye!" said Jack while they all rehashed the affair. "I don't believe it. The gun business is too much for me to swallow."

"The powder you mean?" asked Wilbur.

"Yes, that and the two guns."

"And the peritonitis, the Murphy button—oh Hell, the damn thing has me. All we have are contradictions and coincidences."

"I don't know what to do. I haven't even a suggestion."

"The aquaplane might take us somewhere. But no one saw it, we haven't the number and God knows where it may have come from. They fly long distances. It might be possible to trace it, though, but it's a lot of work. After we did it we might find it had nothing to do with the case at hand in spite of the fact that it may have seemed to be linked with it."

"I've an idea," said Alice. "I'm not much of a detective but if you figure on taking the time to check up on all the planes in the country I believe my idea is worthwhile, quick and positive."

"What's the idea, Alice?" asked Wilbur. "Spring it. I'm willing to grasp at a straw."

"Morley had an operation some place. It took place in some hospital. It was done recently. It probably wasn't done a thousand miles away. It ought to be very easy to check up on it and trace Morley," Alice suggested.

"That's good. That's fine," replied Wilbur. "But supposing he used an assumed name."

"All right, supposing he did," replied Alice proudly. "I told you I was going to do a little sleuthing myself. Well, I did. I went to Doctor Shaw's office and he gave me access to his medical library. I read surgery all afternoon, more particularly abdominal surgery and I think I learned a great deal. Now get this! Murphy buttons are seldom used by surgeons any more. Most of them suture the intestine to the stomach when doing their gastroenterostomies. But there are a few surgeons who still cling to the button. It ought to be an easy matter to find the surgeons who do and check up on their operations. All operations have case records. Whenever you find a gastroenterostomy which has been done lately with a Murphy button, show a photograph of Morley to the surgeon and operating nurses. They'll recognize him. From my reading I gather these patients are under observation some time before they are operated upon, having X-ray pictures and stomach tests done—long enough for the surgeons to become acquainted with their features. And Morley was a person not easily forgotten once he was seen."

"Hum! Damn! That is an idea. Splendid!"

"It may take considerable time to check all of the surgeons but I don't believe that will be necessary. The operation was undoubtedly done in some large institution where a surgeon of some reputation officiated. That sounds awkward perhaps when I have mentioned the fact that the use of the button is an almost obsolete procedure. Nevertheless there are a few reputable surgeons who still use them. I have learned, too, that the button is used at times by those surgeons who suture when the condition of the patient gives the surgeon a limited time in which to perform the operation. But you may be almost sure that Morley would not pick out a surgeon of mean ability. I know I would want the best operator I could find if I found it necessary to undergo such a major operation."

"Alice, you're marvelous," said Wilbur who had become intensely interested. "You're a born detective. It will not take long to ascertain the information necessary. The United Medical Association publishes a book in which it lists the names of all surgeons and their specialties. With a list of all surgeons doing stomach surgery it ought to be quite easy to find the one who operated upon Morley. Damn it, I should have thought of that before. We'll be able to find out where

Morley went when he left Summitville and we ought to be able to follow his movements afterward. Glad you made your inquiry, Alice."

"Well, something must be done. The first thing we know we'll all be accused of the entire plot. It's a good thing some people do not know of the shoe prints and that accusing glove. With such circumstantial evidence and a supposed ownership of the cottage it wouldn't be hard to build up a case."

"Oh, but the ownership of the cottage is disproved."

"Yes, thanks to black light. But if you hadn't thought of it and the authorities had found the tracks and the glove we'd be in a pretty pickle."

"Undoubtedly."

"Well, we don't know what else may crop up."

"Never mind, Alice—murder will out."

"Well, I hope so before we are railroaded to the penitentiary. It would seem it hasn't been our fault that we are free. We've been lucky so far."

"I shall set out on a tour of interrogation of surgeons just as soon as I finish up with my work here. I want to learn the results of the interrogation of Finlay. I want to question the uncle of the Morleys and learn if there is any trace of LaVell. There's a wholesale drug house in Central City and they undoubtedly have a copy of the United Medical Association's book. We can begin there. The line of investigation holds promise."

An interrogation of the Morleys' uncle amounted to nothing. The uncle was an old man in the eighties, incapable of even contemplating a criminal act. He was tottering and almost childish. A report from Loomis gave little promise that anything would be forthcoming from Finlay. He had shut up like a clam and would say nothing about anything. There wasn't a trace of LaVell. No one had seen him, he hadn't returned and his funeral parlors were closed. The uncle had sought the services of another undertaker and the bodies of the Morleys had been buried. With such a jigsaw puzzle upon his hands, Wilbur set forth on his trip of interrogation.

It seemed the only course he could pursue. If that failed there remained the bare possibility that the plane ownership could be established and that it would lead to something. If a search for the plane failed there seemed to be nothing more that could be done. The Morley case would be either an unsolved crime or a suicide.

At Central City Wilbur found the wholesale drug company. They possessed the directory of physicians and surgeons compiled by the United Medical Association. It was a matter of little work to list all the surgeons, especially surgeons doing gastric surgery. The list comprised those in the state to which Central City and Summitville belonged and those in the surrounding states.

"I hardly think Morley would go a great distance," Wilbur remarked as he finished his tabulation. "Chicago is a great surgical center and a world famous clinic is in the territory I have selected. I believe a careful combing of our list will result in something. Now for the search. You can proceed with me or return to Summitville and carry on. Just as you choose. I'm taking the first train out of here for Chicago. Morley, according to my ideas, would either go there or to the world famous clinic."

"I'll go along. I'm intensely interested and don't want to miss anything," answered Jack. "I'll telephone Alice and we'll be on our way."

Haughton called his wife, informed her of their plans and where she could reach them. Within an hour after the telephone communication both men were on a fast train bound for Chicago.

CHAPTER XVI

PELLETIERES' FUNERAL HOME

IN CHICAGO Wilbur sought out the foremost general surgeon and explained his mission. The surgeon culled Wilbur's list further. As a result when the surgeon was through, Wilbur had a rather small list which included only those surgeons who used the Murphy button at all times and those who used it occasionally as a matter of expediency. Thus armed, along with a late photograph of Eugene Morley, Wilbur and Haughton set forth. It looked as though their procedure would bring results in a relatively short time. But there were unforeseen difficulties encountered at once and their calculations were upset. Instead of resolving into an easy task it became a hard one. The first three surgeons whom they sought to interview were out of town and would be for an indefinite period. Their assistants who remained in charge of their practice either knew nothing of the surgeons' previous work or were reluctant to impart any information. Another remembered performing several gastroenterostomies but could not identify the photograph of Morley as that of any of the patients he had operated upon. One positively identified the photograph as that of a man that he had recently operated upon but the operation had been a kidney operation in place of a gastroenterostomy. Some were too busy to give Wilbur any time and others too self-important to condescend to talk. A few ethically inclined informed the investigator that they would not talk about their cases under any circumstances. A few days of such unproductive investigation gave the task a hopeless aspect.

"These surgeons give me a pain in the neck," Wilbur finally exploded after leaving the office of one of the ethical sort. "You'd think they were the most important people on earth. And their damn ethics! That has always made me sick. You'd think they were the most impeccable people in the world. And still about ninety percent of them are fee-splitters, paying physicians incapable of operating a part of their operating fee for steering patients to them. The damned hypocrites! They won't advertise in a newspaper but they'll bribe a brother practitioner to send them cases to cut up. As a result a lot of the population give up normal appendices, normal thyroids, normal this and normal that. More purity!"

"Why not try the hospitals?" suggested Jack.

"That will be much better," said Wilbur. "We should have done that in the first place. They'll not be so damned independent."

And so Wilbur and Haughton began their rounds of various hospitals in the hope that they would discover a record of Morley's operation. They came home exhausted that evening. The hospitals had been more easy of approach but the information obtained was of no value.

"By the Gods," said Wilbur, "I never knew so many people lost their 'innards' before. Armour and Company have nothing on these hospitals. Boy, they slaughter 'em."

"Yes, sir!" replied Jack. "There are more people lacking in anatomy than I ever dreamed of. If the slaughter is general, and I suppose it is, it isn't going to be long until the side shows will reverse their tactics. Instead of showing someone with three legs, one eye or two heads, they'll be charging admission to see a guy with all his God-given things intact. A bird with both tonsils will be able to make a living by simply opening his mouth and saying 'Ah.' A woman without a scar on her belly will command more attention than a tattooed lady."

"The human race is decaying."

"I believe it."

The records of hospital after hospital were combed. The photograph of Morley was exhibited in the hope that someone would recognize it. No one did. The name Morley was not found on any of the registers. This might be expected, however, because he might have entered a hospital under an assumed name. Finally when Wilbur had almost decided that Morley's surgery had not been done in Chicago a hospital furnished a clue. It was the private institution of a celebrated surgeon. The surgeon himself was not at hand but a surgical nurse, an assistant operator, gave the information.

"Yes, Mr. Wilbur," said she. "We operated a man for a gastric ulcer some time ago—about the time you suggest. The reason I recall it is because it was the only gastroen- terostomy we have done in some time. We do not specialize in them, although we usually do a number of them every month. It just so happens, however, that for some period we have done no gastric surgery except this one case. The doctor uses the oblong Murphy button exclusively. You see Dr. Murphy was one of his Gods."

"Would you recognize a photograph of the patient?" asked Wilbur as he produced Morley's picture.

"I don't know that I could," replied the nurse as she looked at the photograph. "You see I only saw the patient in the operating room. The nurse who attended him undoubt- edly would. I can find out who she was if you wish."

"Do you know whether the patient wore dental plates?"

"Yes, I remember that. I recall the fact because the anes- thetist failed to take them out before beginning the ether. The patient took the anesthetic badly and nearly swallowed the plates."

"Will your records show where this patient came from?"

"Oh, yes. I'll give you all the details if you care to have them."

"I wish you would," said Wilbur. "Your information is the most promising that I have unearthed in a thorough scouring of all the city hospitals. In fact it is the only operation I have discovered where a Murphy button was used. Of course I refer to those done within a certain definite period."

Wilbur and Haughton accompanied the nurse to an in- dexed file of the patients' names, their operations, residences and complete histories. After some little delay she found a record of the case in question.

"Here it is," said she. "The name is William Scott. His address was 1648 DeVon Place."

"That's very good," replied Wilbur. "The name may amount to nothing as the party we are seeking to locate might have had a very good reason to hide his identity. Have you any more information about Mr. Scott? Did he pass the button?"

"Oh, the patient died, Mr. Wilbur," replied the nurse.

"Died!" exclaimed Wilbur.

"Oh, yes. I thought you understood that. Here's the record. Read it for yourself."

Wilbur took the record and read the salient points of the case which interested him: "Gastroenterostomy performed for ulcer—ulcer removed—lethal termination fifteenth day from septic peritonitis which set in tenth day."

"Hum!" said Wilbur as he handed the record back to the nurse. "Strange! Could you call the nurse on the case?"

"Let's see," replied the surgical nurse as she glanced at the case history. "Yes. It was Miss Peoples. She's on another case right now. I'll call her."

The nurse left and returned a few moments later with Miss Peoples whom she introduced.

"Might I trouble you a moment, Miss Peoples?" said Wilbur as he showed her the photograph of Eugene Morley. "Is this a photograph of Mr. Scott, whom you nursed?"

"I believe so," replied Miss Peoples. "The photograph strongly resembles the patient."

"Mr. Scott died in the hospital, I suppose?" said Wilbur to the surgical nurse.

"Yes, sir."

"Then I suppose an undertaker called for the body?"

"Yes, sir."

"Could you tell me what undertaker removed the remains?"

"Yes, sir," replied the nurse as she consulted the records again. "Pelletieres' Undertaking Company."

"Thanks very much for your information," said Wilbur as he and Haughton took their leave.

"Looks hot!" said Haughton outside.

"I'm not so sure," replied Wilbur. "It might be another co-incidence. Dead! Hum! And yet someone may have put those two holes in Morley's body to avert a suspicion against themselves. It wasn't possible to find out whether the body was shot before or after death on account of the decomposition. Anyhow we're bound for Pelletieres'."

"O.K.," replied Jack. "But it sounds asinine to me, this shooting after death."

"This is an asinine case," Wilbur laughed. "It will have to be solved in an asinine manner.

"Well, we've started to run the thread from Morley's operation. We must proceed. This is the first information even to lead us anywhere. Except for the name everything checks. Mr. Scott died from a septic peritonitis, his operation was a gastroenterostomy and the button did not pass. We must exhaust the possibilities before proceeding further. If Mr. Scott was not Mr. Morley, we'll be going other places and seeing other things. And remember, Jack, it was your wife who suggested this procedure."

"Yeah! She suggested that we buy the cottage on Ramona Lake too. If it hadn't been for her I'd never have known anything about the Morley case and you wouldn't either."

"Well, I'm rather glad she intrigued you into buying the place," replied Wilbur. "It's been the means of putting me on a very interesting case."

"A baffling one, if that's what you mean."

Pelletieres' was a huge city establishment where the business of burying the dead was run on a modern basis. They went on the theory of volume and decreased the cost accordingly. There were numerous branches throughout the city. Wilbur and Haughton sought the fountainhead, of course. Wilbur surveyed the place, the advertising upon the windows and three funeral cars parked at the curbing.

"It looks like the shuffling-off process was a big business," said he.

"It appears so," returned Jack. "A very comforting sight for the well, wouldn't you say?"

"It makes me think. With such a number of corpses as they must have all the time, it occurs to me that it might be an easy matter to forget one now and then. You get my idea?"

"Oh, that's hardly possible, I should think. Death certificates have to be signed, go through a certain form, burial permits issued, etc."

"Oh yeah. There's more than one way to kill a cat, too. But let's step inside."

The interior of Pelletieres' was furnished in exquisite taste—the rugs, hangings, flower pots and lighting. While waiting for an attendant Wilbur and Haughton admired the decorations, and reverently inspected the caskets which were on display. "Gruesome," said Jack, "shopping for caskets." Wilbur was inspecting one minutely.

"Oh ho!" said he. "This is a duplicate of the coffin which contained the corpse of Morley." A moment later he exclaimed, "It is! Look at the label—the Summitville Casket Company."

Haughton stooped and read the inscription, "Oh, well, that doesn't mean much," said he. "The Summitville Casket Company is quite a large affair and is probably well known to undertakers. I imagine morticians buy from all companies at some time in their career."

"Maybe so."

At that instant an attendant approached.

"Is there anything I can do for you gentlemen?" said he. He wore a large white chrysanthemum in the buttonhole of his black suit—an undertaker's habit.

"I'd like to speak to Mr. Pelletiere," answered Wilbur, "when he isn't busy."

"Did you want to see any one of the brothers in particular?" smiled the attendant. "There are three of us. I am one."

"Oh, I beg your pardon," returned Wilbur. "I didn't know there were three of you. Of course, you will do."

"Step this way, gentlemen," Mr. Pelletiere said graciously. He led them into a private office in the back. Within the room he pointed to some very comfortable chairs and remarked, "Be seated, gentlemen." He seated himself and then asked, "And now of what service can I be to you?"

"Mr. Pelletiere, I am an investigator," Wilbur explained. "I am wondering if you have any recollection of burying a man by the name of Scott—William Scott, of 1648 DeVon Place?"

"Oh, I recall it very vividly. The Scotts are very prominent people. We are conducting a funeral for Mrs. Scott tomorrow. Her brother just passed away."

"Then you actually buried Mr. Scott?"

"We most certainly did."

"Another bum hunch," said Jack.

"Oh, I don't know," replied Wilbur quickly, and then turned to Mr. Pelletiere. "Do you know this of your own knowledge, Mr. Pelletiere?"

"Well, we secured the body at the hospital, placed it in a coffin and delivered it to the grave," replied Mr. Pelletiere. "There was no embalming done. Mrs. Scott objected. We did not actually conduct the funeral either. Some out-of-town undertaker did that—someone, I believe, from Mrs. Scott's home town."

"Do you know who it was?"

"I do not. Mrs. Scott could tell you, though."

"You have no record?"

"There would hardly be any record since we did the actual burying. However, I'll consult the office records and see if there is any mention of it."

"I wish you would," replied Wilbur.

The undertaker left the office.

"Do you see what I see?" asked Haughton after Pelletiere was gone.

"I see nothing strange," replied Wilbur.

"Well, cast your eye into the waste basket."

Wilbur looked into the waste basket and saw the object of Haughton's scrutiny. He reached into the basket and pulled out the object.

"Careless to say the least," Wilbur remarked. "Not at all in harmony with a funeral home."

"Same old Summitville brand."

"Yeah, Coon Hollow!"

Wilbur dropped the empty bottle back into the basket. A moment later Mr. Pelletiere returned.

"There is no notation of the out-of-town undertaker's name," said Mr. Pelletiere upon his entrance. "The matter is really inconsequential, however, since we did the actual burying. The matter of the conduction was just a whim of Mrs. Scott. You know some people are very sentimental."

"Very well," said Wilbur. "Did I understand you to say that you were burying Mrs. Scott's brother tomorrow?"

"Yes, sir. The poor woman seems to have had her troubles all at once."

"That is rather a load of grief," answered Wilbur. "What ailed the brother?"

"Ptomaine poisoning. He suffered terribly, so they say."

"Hum!" Wilbur grunted in bewilderment and then said, "Well, thanks for your information. We'll not trouble you further."

"If I have been of any assistance to you I am very glad."

"You've probably helped to mess our affair up further, but it's not your fault."

After leaving the Pelletieres', Wilbur and Haughton sought their hotel. There was nothing more that could be done. It would have been a desecration to have invaded the Scott home to investigate further while it housed the dead body of Mrs. Scott's brother. Besides it wouldn't be fair to question her in her hour of grief.

"I can't see that we are getting any place," Haughton said when they were in their room. "It would appear that we're on a wild goose chase."

"It would but for one thing," replied Wilbur. "That is the conduction of the funeral. An out-of-town undertaker doesn't sound right to me. It may have been a whim. I know there are those sentimental fools. But that's strange and unusual, and whenever I find anything strange and unusual I'm inquisitive. The date of the death of her husband almost corresponds with the date of the death of Morley. You'll say that's another coincidence, I know. But that's grounded in me so indelibly that I can't shake it off. I don't believe in them. Now! I intend watching the Scott house from now on until after the brother's funeral. If Mrs. Scott had an out-of-town undertaker conduct her husband's funeral for sentimental reasons, I wonder if he won't conduct the brother's. I wish I had asked Mr. Pelletiere whether that would be the case."

"Your mind is on LaVell."

"Sure it is. I think he was the undertaker. I don't know why except for the association of everything."

"Well, if you want to know what I think, I think this little jaunt is going to end just like the other things terminated— the clues, the autopsies, etc."

"I won't say that it won't, Jack," replied Wilbur. "But I have my own idea."

"What is your idea?"

"Morley might have been leading a dual life. He might have been Scott here in the city and Morley in Summitville."

"That's possible."

"That might explain the undertaker."

"Hum! Damn it, that's right. Say—your mind works fast."

"Oh, that's not smart. It's just a supposition. I may be wrong."

"Hum!" grunted Jack. "Say! The undertaker said these Scotts were somebody. I wonder what he did for a living."

"That's an idea. Where's the telephone book or a city directory?"

Haughton produced the telephone book and Wilbur hastily leafed the book to the S's.

"Here it is," said he. "William Scott, general agent for Nivorsky Amphibians."

"The devil! An aquaplane salesman!"

"Sure as you're born. We're hot, Jack. We're hot. Scott's plane on the lake—say!"

"Right!"

"The Morley case is sizzling, if you ask me."

"That's one! Morley leading a double life! But that only takes us in deeper. More motives and other suspects. Mrs. Scott! But, say, she buried Scott."

"Maybe she did," Wilbur said laconically.

"Oh, I see!"

"That's where the out-of-town undertaker comes in."

"I've got you."

"A conspiracy between LaVell and Mrs. Scott."

"Sure! Sure!"

"That would explain Mrs. Morley's death."

"Certainly. There'd be a reason for wanting her out of the way. Jeez! Wilbur, this is a deep-dyed plot."

"It's a clever thing."

"And right while we're discussing the whole affair I believe there's a connection between the Pelletiere Undertaking Company and the City of Summitville. The links in this chain fit too well."

"I've been thinking about that too. But we can't be too rash. The liquor might have been a gift of old man Tully to the Pelletieres."

"But if you'll remember old man Tully said he knew nothing about liquor."

"So he did. But he may have lied. I can tell you that the moon is made out of green cheese but that doesn't necessarily mean that I don't know better."

"It's a funny mess."

"My mind is made up anyhow," Wilbur stated. "You remain here at the hotel. I'm going to shadow the house on DeVon Place. I may learn much to question the widow about later."

CHAPTER XVII

A SCOTCH FUNERAL

THE SCOTT HOME on DeVon Place surprised Wilbur. It was in a highly restricted district, a dark brown structure of modern design set well back in grounds of magnitude. No other homes were near it. The grounds were excellently land-scaped. In all, the place was pretentious. The undertaker had spoken the truth. The Scotts were somebody.

From a vantage point Wilbur watched the place all after-noon and night. But no one came or went. Not even a mes-senger boy arrived. To all appearances the place was deserted and there was no one who even cared to inquire about the funeral or send a message of condolence. A strange, incon-gruous situation.

"The strangest thing I ever saw or heard of," Wilbur said to himself. "No flowers delivered! No condolences! No call-ers! Nobody!"

The vigil of the following morning proved as fruitless as that before. The undertakers didn't even appear on the scene. The flower spray upon the door was the only sign that there was anything extraordinary about the place except its evident luxury. No one entered and no one left. At two o'clock in the afternoon a lone person appeared—a minister. He walked slowly into the house. Some little time after a motor hearse of Pelletieres' pulled into the drive, followed by a single cab. And then to Wilbur's complete consternation about twenty minutes later a casket was wheeled out of the house and two of the Pelletieres placed it in the hearse. No pallbearers! An extremely simple funeral! Another whim of Mrs. Scott! The minister escorted a heavily black veiled and weeping lady to the lone cab and the funeral cortege was complete. The hearse moved off, the cab followed and Wilbur watched them disappear down the wide drive of DeVon Place.

"Well, I'll be damned," was all the criminologist could say. He wheeled about, walked a few blocks and hailed a passing cab. Later at the hotel he said to Haughton, "Damned uncommunicative, these Scotts. But they may have the nationality as well as the name."

"What's the trouble?" asked Haughton.

"Their funerals are banal—a hearse and one car. No flowers; no one attended but the sky pilot and the widow. Her weeds prevented my getting a squint at her. There was no sign of LaVell."

"Hum!" exclaimed Jack. "Damned mysterious!"

"It's a nutty business."

"It must have been a strictly private funeral."

"More than private—frugal if you ask me. That's another thing I don't like besides coincidences—frugality with evidence of pomp."

"Well, while you've been on your little funeral attendance I've done a little work. Sitting around here waiting on you became a bore. I went to the office of the Nivorsky agent."

"Good!"

"Hold everything! Not so good! It's a room and nothing more. The name is on the door, there's some dumb advertising that litters the floor along with cigarette butts, and a desk with a lot of rings on the top of it."

"Which spells?"

"I don't know."

"Don't be dumb all of your life, Jack. It's a blind. It's a bootlegging office."

"I believe you're right. That explains the ship. There's only one. It's riding the waves at the Atlas Yacht Club. I ran down there and took a look at it. It's equipped for night flying. I inquired about a bit and gathered the impression that it was a 'rummer.'"

"It explains the wealth of Scott on that information. How large is the ship?"

"Good sized, tri-motored with a large cabin."

"It would carry a corpse?"

"A couple and then some."

"Did you learn any more?"

"Not much."

"Meaning which?"

"I went to Pelletieres', found the fellow that drove the funeral car at Scott's funeral. They buried him at Rose Lawn."

"Not so good!" answered Wilbur. "Did you try the bell hop out?"

"You bet! I did that."

"Any luck?"

"Plenty."

"Good boy. How is the stuff?"

"Try it."

Haughton reached in his grip, brought forth a bottle and handed it to Wilbur.

"Well, I'll be damned!" exclaimed Wilbur as he held it up. "Coon Hollow!"

"Nothing else but. And guess where it came from."

"Search me!"

"Pelletieres'!"

"Holy Mackerel!" exploded Wilbur as he took a gulp. "What a sweet case this is."

CHAPTER XVIII

LITTLE GRAINS OF SAND

THE NEXT DAY Wilbur and Haughton sought to interview the widow of the late William Scott. They found no one at home. The blinds were pulled, the doors were locked and there was no sign of life about. Evidently Mrs. Scott had packed up and left. The grief occasioned by her husband's death and that of the brother had overcome her.

"Let's go in anyhow," said Wilbur as he fished a bunch of keys from his pocket. "This lock doesn't look tough and I think I have a key that will do the trick."

"I'm with you if you want to try it," answered Jack. "The place is secluded and no one will know."

"We'll have a peek anyhow," said Wilbur as he passed a likely looking key into the lock and opened the door at once.

Looking up and down the street and seeing no one, both men entered the Scott home and closed the door after them. The interior of the home was tastefully decorated. They entered directly into a large living room which extended entirely across the front of the house. Two photographs on the mantel immediately engaged Wilbur's attention. One, that of a man, was trimmed in black. It was not a photograph of Eugene Morley and was evidently a picture of William Scott. The other was a picture of a woman—probably Mrs. Scott. Wilbur scrutinized both photographs intently. After doing so he went hurriedly from room to room and scanned everything. He missed nothing with his practiced eye. In a bedroom he picked up a pair of earrings. He was just about to leave the room after doing that when he noted something else sticking out from under the bed.

"Well, I'll be damned," said he as he stooped and picked up a pair of lady's shoes, whose right heel and left sole were worn off exactly as Alice Haughton's were. And as he examined them closely he found Ramona Lake sand in front of the heel.

"Hum! Damn!" Wilbur said over and over again as he examined the shoes. Finally he tossed them under the bed.

Nothing more of consequence rewarded their search. They emerged from the house as they had entered.

"Something's transpired," said Jack after they had left the house. "What's purring?"

"Plenty," Wilbur answered. "I've almost got the heebie-jeebies. The solution is in my hand but it's so crazy I can't tell it. We're on the track though. The supposition that Morley led a double life is more evident.

"I don't want you to laugh at me. There is nothing concrete. I almost doubt my own deductions. Just hold on. The non-essentials, the seeming inconsequential things in this case, are beginning to tell."

"You mean ladies' shoes, earrings, and what have you? God knows you have enough."

"That's it exactly."

"What are you going to do?"

"I'm going to wait until Mrs. Scott returns. I think I'll be able to burst this case wide open."

CHAPTER XIX

A FATAL INTERVIEW

SINCE MRS. SCOTT'S ABSENCE from her home promised to be of some duration, Jack returned to Summittville. He would gather what he could of information in that place. And Alice could not be left alone for an indefinite period. Wilbur remained in Chicago, watching, and waiting for the return of Mrs. Scott. For weeks neither Haughton nor Wilbur learned anything to their advantage. And then at last at the end of eight weeks Wilbur got a rumble. There were signs of life appearing at the Scott home. Mrs. Scott had returned. Ascertaining this fact, Wilbur called upon the city detective bureau and enlisted aid, little knowing why he did so at the time unless he reasoned that another person would be present when he interviewed Mrs. Scott and thereby prove her statements. As it turned out it was very well that he did. Detective Clarke, a very able man, was assigned to accompany him by the Chief of Detectives. Both men arrived at the Scott residence about the hour of noon. A maid met them at the door.

"Who shall I say is calling?" asked the maid.

"Mr. Rodney of the Nivorsky Company," answered Wilbur as he handed her a duplicate card of the president of the Nivorsky Company. "It's about the seaplane."

The maid turned to take the card to her mistress. Both Wilbur and Clarke entered without waiting for an invitation to come in. In a few moments Mrs. Scott entered the living room.

"Mr. Rodney?" said she as she advanced.

"Mrs. Scott," answered Wilbur as he held forth his hand in greeting. Turning toward Clarke he went on, "Mrs. Scott, Mr. Clarke, our new Chicago representative."

"I'm very glad to meet you, Mr. Clarke," returned the elegant Mrs. Scott.

Wilbur studied Mrs. Scott very intently.

"Won't you sit down, gentlemen?" said she as she graciously pointed out some elegantly upholstered chairs.

Wilbur and Clarke seated themselves, as did Mrs. Scott.

"You'll pardon our calling right at the luncheon hour I'm sure," said Wilbur. "But my time is very precious; in fact I have remained in the city a longer time now than I expected, thinking you would return day after day."

"I'm very sorry," said she pleasantly.

"I was very much grieved to learn of your husband's death. I knew him very well, jolly sort. I never dreamed that he ever suffered from any stomach disorder."

"Oh yes. He had been bothered for years—just endured. You know how these high-strung energetic men are—they never give up until they have to. He endured until he could stand it no longer. The doctors assured him that his operation would be a success and of course he believed them. They operated. Well, the operation was a success I guess, but peritonitis set in. You know the rest. They seldom recover from it, so I'm told. You wanted to talk to me about the seaplane, I suppose? I'd like to dispose of it. A woman could hardly carry on and I do not care to take up flying."

"Oh, there are many other hazardous occupations," Wilbur replied somewhat pointedly.

"Oh, I dare say flying is quite safe but I just have a natural timidity. I don't think I could ever scrape up the courage."

"I would imagine that. You never flew with your husband?"

"Oh dear no! I never had the slightest inclination."

"But you do have courage, Mrs. Morley," Wilbur said suddenly.

"Mrs. Morley!"

"You did not misunderstand me. I said Mrs. Morley," replied Wilbur with a grin that was almost sardonic. "You are no more Mrs. Scott than I am Mr. Rodney of the Nivorsky

Corporation. I am Lyman K. Wilbur, an investigator for the Bankers' Indemnity Company."

"Why—why—you're mistaken. The very impertinence! And in my own house. You'll hear from this. The very idea! The absurdity. I'll sue you."

"I hardly think you will, Mrs. Morley. It is very rare that people start suits in the place you are soon going to be. Are these your earrings?"

Wilbur reached in his pocket as he arose and withdrew a pair of earrings. He walked over to where the lady sat and handed them to her. He smiled curiously.

"Why, ah—yes, of course," she stammered after she had taken them nervously, examined them and paled.

"Very well," replied Wilbur as she gave back the earrings.

"We'll let the matter of the earrings go for the moment. Is the picture of the lady upon the mantel yours, Mrs. Morley?"

"That's my picture—but you are talking to Mrs. Scott, if you please."

"You think the picture belongs to you. I was not asking about the ownership though. My question might have been a bit ambiguous. I meant to ask if it was supposed to be a likeness of yourself."

"Say, what in the world is the matter with you? Of course it is. Anyone can see that it is."

"I rather suspected the contrary," Wilbur replied cannily. "I would put it this way—you are a very good likeness of the picture."

"Just what do you mean? I'm not going to stand for all of this nonsense. That is a photograph of myself and the earrings you have are mine. What is the big idea?"

Clarke, whose sense of hearing was very acute, thought he heard a noise in some other part of the house. He arose from his seat and cocked his ear for any further sound.

"You are a very splendid likeness of the picture, Mrs. Morley," Wilbur came to the point. "The operator did very well. He's a clever man. The dimples have been made perfectly. The lifting has been exquisite. The staining of the iris in each eye is flawless. The chlorine has made your raven hair a marvelous bright chestnut. All of your work shows the mark of a craftsman but for one thing. Your beauty surgeon could not put the mole upon your neck. Or if he could you failed to tell him about it. You should wear a dress with a high neck. If you'll notice the photograph shows that Mrs. Scott had a rather pronounced nevus on her neck."

"You! You! You dirty rat!" Mrs. Morley raged. "Get out of my house! Go! Get! I'll call an officer!"

"I am at your service, Madam," said Clarke at this moment. "I will accommodate you. I am detective Clarke of the City Detective Bureau."

Clarke pulled back his coat to show his badge of authority.

"Oh! Oh!" Mrs. Morley cried in anger. "I always have heard that detectives were monsters. Now I know it!"

"And the earrings, if you will notice, Mrs. Morley, are not the clasp kind," said Wilbur as he juggled them together upon the palm of his hand. "They have been worn by a woman whose ears were pierced. Yours, I notice, have not been pierced."

"Ugh!" cried Mrs. Morley with a feline expression upon her face, her hands upraised and claw-like. "I could scratch your eyes out."

"I do not doubt your animosity. You have very good cause to have a burning hatred for me. But to go on, the shoes in Mrs. Scott's bedroom are peculiar. The heel of the right one is run over and the sole of the left one worn off. In front of the heel of each shoe there is a peculiar colored sand. It's Ramona Lake sand, Mrs. Morley."

Slowly, easily, quietly the dining-room door which led into the living-room was opening. First a mere slit appeared, then a crack—the hinge creaked. Clarke whirled, jerked his police special from his shoulder holster and pointed it at the door. He was not a moment too quick. The blue barrel of an automatic pointed at him as the door suddenly swung wide open. Clarke fired. The blue barreled automatic fell as it discharged and the bullet went wild. Clarke's gun barked again. The man who had held the automatic clutched savagely at his breast, pitched forward on the floor and rolled over.

"Oh, my God! Eugene! Eugene!" cried Mrs. Morley as she dashed past Wilbur to hold Eugene Morley's head in her arms for the last few moments she would ever do so.

Eugene Morley looked up into his wife's eyes pitifully. "We might have known," he gasped. "May God have mercy on you. I should never have forced you into it. Good-bye and God bless you."

After a few moments the hysterical, almost maniacal Mrs. Morley was taken away by detective Clarke. Wilbur remained with the dead man.

CHAPTER XX

THE END OF AN ALMOST PERFECT CRIME

LATER AT THE HOTEL Wilbur put in a call to Summitville.

"Hello, Jack!" said he when Haughton answered. "How are tricks?"

"Oh, just about the same. Nothing from Loomis. Nothing new. There's still plenty of Coon Hollow, however. What do you know?"

"Well, get a load of this. I know who killed Eugene Morley."

"It wasn't a suicide?"

"I'll say it wasn't. He was shot."

"The devil! Who shot him?"

"A detective by the name of Clarke. He's on the Chicago city force. He's a damn good shot too, I'm here to tell."

"Aw, Hell! You're kidding."

"I'm not kidding. I just saw him do the little job a short while ago. And that isn't all the big news either. Mrs. Morley is now sojourning in a little barred room. She's having a little informal chat with the police matron at this moment."

"Aw, Hell! Wilbur, you're kidding."

"I'm not kidding. Get in your car and run up. See for yourself. Or I've a better idea. Hop over to Central City and take a plane. Bring Alice with you. How is she? Pardon my not asking sooner."

"She's just fine. But honest, Lyman, what is the lowdown?"

"Just what I said. I'll tell you all about it when you arrive. Don't forget to bring plenty of your important belongings."

"I'll do that little thing and hop over as soon as it is humanly possible."

In Summitville Jack and Alice were completely dumb-founded. They were tense with excitement. Wilbur's message was unbelievable. Both gave little credence to the truth of his assertions. It was probably a prank; maybe just a ruse to have them come into the city for a party. But no matter. Incredible as it all seemed, they packed their bags and plenty of their most important belongings. In a short time they were on their way to Central City. At that city's airport they took an outgoing plane for Chicago.

While Haughton and his wife were winging their way, Wilbur went to the central police station to interview Mrs. Morley. There were many things requiring an explanation.

The police matron had succeeded in composing Mrs. Morley by the time Wilbur arrived at the station. More than that, Mrs. Morley was willing to talk freely after Wilbur informed her that he would intercede in her behalf if she did. He had heard her husband's dying words and knew that her part in the whole ghastly affair was largely forced. He gathered his information. When he had done so the Morley case and the strange city of Summitville were an open book. Leaving her Wilbur said to himself, "What a whale of a story for Alice and Jack. Hum! Damn it all, it sounds like a fairy tale except that it's gruesome. And I thought all the crime was hatched in large cities."

Haughton and his wife arrived in Chicago in a tri-motored Ford, and lost no time in getting from the airport to the hotel where Wilbur was stopping. They secured a room adjoining Wilbur's. Alice curled herself upon the bed and Jack unpacked the grips. Jack brought forth their most important belongings. Wilbur fetched ginger ale from his own room and a little liquid nourishment was indulged in by all. Jack then sprawled across the foot of the bed and Wilbur took his position in a chair which was opposite.

"Well, let's have the fairy tale," said Alice. "I'm dying to listen."

"This *is* a story," Wilbur began. "It's a story of a man with brains. It's a story that might never have been told. Only the screwy nature of Fate gives me the pleasure of recounting the tale. It's not one of brilliant detection. It's not the brainy deduction one finds in the dick novels. It's really a happen-so."

"Well, go on, Lyman," urged Alice as she shifted restlessly upon the bed. "Don't waste time with a prologue."

"This story, the entire tale, is a fashion plate of crime conceived in the brain of Eugene Morley. He concocted a scheme to become a rich man with little effort. It was diabolical, cunning, daring in its execution and almost successful. Had it not been for a few frayed ends in the weave of his criminal cloth this story would never have been told."

"Well, go on, Lyman," said Alice. "Get into your story."

"All right, Mrs. Haughton," returned Wilbur. "I think I'll be able to do that after just one more little immersion."

The second highball provoked the telling of the tale.

"If you will remember," Wilbur continued, after draining his glass, "there was a story that Eugene Morley philandered with some woman last summer who was vacationing on Ramona Lake. You'll recall that we traced the rumor but put it down as an old wives' tale. There was a woman at Ramona Lake, but no one knew who she was or where she came from. The fact is we couldn't have found out who she was. She went under an assumed name since she was taking one of those little perennial jaunts that some wives take to avoid a constant life with a man who grows distasteful every so often. In other words, as they say, 'She left her husband,' In some way or another Morley met her. Of course there are many ways to accomplish such an end. They conversed, brought up the past and found that they had both seen the light of day in the same little New England town.

" 'Why, you're not Eugene Morley?' said the surprised woman. 'I am Gene Morley,' he answered. 'Well, I'll tell you the truth. I am not Mrs. Brown. I am really Mrs. Scott. But my maiden name was Lucille Starrett.' 'Lucille Starrett!' exclaimed Morley. 'Well as I live and breathe.' They had been childhood sweethearts. You can imagine no doubt what happened. It's an old story. Morley, who was having difficulties with his wife at the time, capitulated before her shrine. Two kindred spirits embarked on the ship of consolation which shipped to a clandestine port. Enough! The summer season closed at Ramona Lake. The woman returned to her husband as a great number of errant wives do and Morley 'made up' with his wife. The affair passed as a summer's flirtation for the woman, but not as such for Morley. He had learned a great deal. The woman's husband was wealthy. He had made a fortune in the peculiar manner that many have been made in, in the last ten years. He acted as an agent for the Nivorsky Amphibian. That was a blind for his real occupation. Incidentally he liked flying. Eugene Morley, the introspective, the close observer, also saw that this woman strongly resembled his wife. That may have been the reason for his infatuation for her as a married woman and it may have been the reason for his childhood admiration of her. They say a man falls for a particular type. I cannot say. That's beyond the realm of my occupation. But no matter. This woman, the woman to whom he was attracted, was the wife of a man named William Scott, the man with the wealth. Suddenly William Scott died from an operation—a gastroenterostomy. Mrs. Scott had not forgotten Morley. In her extremity, in her grief, she sent the word of her husband's passing to Morley. The thing Morley had been waiting for had occurred. And thus did Fate deliver the incentive for Morley's nefarious scheme. His mind worked rapidly after receiving this word from Mrs. Scott. He went to Central City and wired her that he was coming to her. She believed his sincerity. And now let me introduce Pierre LaVell. He was very close to Morley. In fact he was so very close that he was under deep obligations to Morley since the cashier had seen that he obtained large loans on illegitimate paper. Morley explained his plan to LaVell. He told him that he would receive half of the money he expected to get out of his scheme if it was successful. LaVell fell for it. He virtually had to do as Morley told him. At this time Morley had embezzled some money from the Summitville bank. He had taken out his life insurance years before. He figured to take all there was in the bank. Whole hog or none for him. And he didn't intend to miss the insurance. After getting LaVell into the scheme he told his wife of his peculations, how she would secure the insurance money, how she would fit into his murderous scheme. She was frantic, wild, because she was madly in love with Eugene Morley. But rather than lose her husband, who meant more to her than her own life, by telling the authorities of his plans, she fell into his scheme. She did this even after he had told her of his *affaire d'amour* with Mrs. Scott. Imagine a woman who cared that much."

"Well, I care that much for Jack," said Alice, who was now sitting up in the bed and listening with an intensity. "I'm for Mrs. Morley."

"You care, Alice, but I don't believe you would let him do what Eugene Morley did," answered Wilbur.

"I'm beginning to see things," said Jack as he lit a cigarette and passed his pack to Wilbur.

"Oh, you only think so," replied Wilbur. "The story isn't half told. Let's have another little snifter and then I'll go on. I've talked so much now my lips are parched."

Alice jumped out of bed and did the honors so that no time would be lost in the story telling. After that, while they all sipped at their drinks, Wilbur went on. "So with his accessories willing and ready to carry out his plan, Morley went on," said he. "He and Pierre LaVell left for Chicago. In this city they went direct to the Scott home. The ingenious Morley relied upon his mastery of the widow. He stirred the ember of the previous summer. He more than consoled the poor widow. He told her that his own wife was dead and that he could sympathize with her in her grief on that account. He even went so far as to tell her that he would be willing to marry her as soon as it would seem graceful to do it. He implored her to allow him the pleasure of looking after the details of the funeral. Trusting, a subservient soul, she believed him. Gaining her trust, the first thing he did was to take her with him in a cab to Pelletieres'. There, in her presence, but far enough from her to be unheard, he told the Pelletieres that she desired LaVell to conduct the funeral. He told them that it was just a little matter of sentiment on her part. The

Pelletieres readily consented. Who wouldn't under the circumstances? They had supplied the casket and the funeral
cortege. In fact they were delighted to get away from those
funeral details which require tact and tenderness.

"With this accomplished, Morley took Mrs. Scott home. It
was then that LaVell came upon the scene. He became the
funeral director. This is sordid. But that night when the Scott
household was asleep, LaVell and Morley removed the
corpse of Scott from the casket and substituted weight for the
body. The body was taken by them to the Atlas Yacht Club
and loaded into Scott's own seaplane. Next day LaVell con-
ducted a wonderful funeral over the empty casket; the minister eulogized; much weeping was indulged in and in the end
one hundred and fifty pounds of sand was buried in the
earth."

"Well, I'll be damned!" exclaimed Jack as he gulped
down what was left of his highball.

"And now comes the part where we fell down," Wilbur
continued. "Morley was an expert flier. He was in the air
service during the war. It's strange we never thought of that
possibility when thinking of the aquaplane on Ramona Lake
and it is stranger that no one ever told us about it. But that is
all in the past. The next afternoon he asked Mrs. Scott for
permission to fly the Scott plane. She granted him the permission. He and LaVell flew to Ramona Lake with the
corpse of Scott safely hidden in the fuselage. They landed,
hid the body in the tunnel which led from Bakers Landing to
the Morley cottage and waited. Morley flew the plane back
to Chicago, consoled the widow as only he could and left
her, after informing her that he would return as soon as possible. You can see what happened."

"Right now I've got a vivid mind picture of that blue
serge shank button lying in the boat house," said Jack. "And
as I anticipate the story you were correct about those coming
and going footprints."

"Granted! You're right," Wilbur smiled. "But Morley still
had much to do. He proceeded to disappear. On his arrival in
Summitville he saw to it that money loaned to other banks

was called in. He waited until all the Summitville factory payrolls were in. At the opportune moment he went south with two hundred thousand dollars. He disappeared. Later when Scott's body was thoroughly decomposed he came back after night. He and LaVell went to the cottage to arrange the corpse that was to be taken for that of Morley. And then the blunder! Morley shot the corpse of Scott twice with his own gun. He realized this immediately after, but he knew nothing about ballistics and hadn't the faintest idea that his gun was loaded with black powder while the bank gun was loaded with ballistite. Both guns were of the same caliber so he did what any ordinary thick headed criminal would do under the circumstances: he put the bank's gun beside the body after firing it twice. Why he shot the body through the head and through the heart I don't know unless it was his idea to complicate the case. One shot might have been accidental from fright occasioned by the gruesome deed. In leaving the cottage he either dropped his own gun intentionally at Bakers Landing or lost it."

"Damn it all, you are clever, Wilbur, no foolin'," said Jack.

"Yes, you're real bright," Alice giggled. "Except when it comes to ladies' footwear."

"Oh yeah!" replied Wilbur. "Well, I'll get to that after a time."

"Go on with your story," said Jack. "I didn't mean to interrupt."

"That finishes Morley's disappearance," Wilbur continued. "He returned to Chicago to console the widow. He persuaded her that she needed a rest and suggested that she run down to his cottage for a while. His solicitation was so earnest and pronounced that the poor widow did not decline. On the night that the cottage burned he flew her to Ramona Lake. They landed at Bakers Landing. Morley took her to his cottage. There, believing in his sincerity of purpose, Mrs. Scott joined him in a few drinks of that precious Coon Hollow. Mrs. Morley was instructed to come to the cottage that night. By a prearranged signal she made known her arrival. It was then that Morley induced Mrs. Scott to take a night cap. The drink contained enough arsenic to kill a horse. She passed out quickly from a paralysis of her vital centers. Mrs. Morley entered the cottage after the murder. Morley took her ring from her finger and placed it on the dead woman's finger. He removed the plates from Mrs. Scott's mouth and substituted those of his wife. Then he dragged the inert form into the compartment between the floors, soaked the cottage in oil and departed through the tunnel. Mrs. Morley replaced the cement blocks in the tunnel entrance. Morley closed the end at Bakers Landing when he went out. She fired the cottage after filling the cellar wall and then met her husband at the lake. They entered the plane and flew back to Chicago. The plot was clever, ingenious and bound for success but for one thing—Mrs. Scott's ears were pierced and Mrs. Morley's were not. I noted that when I made my inspection of the dead woman's body."

"Damned clever, Wilbur," said Jack. "Nobody else would do that except you. Now I see why you were so interested in the earrings. A smart bit of detail, I'll say."

"Never mind the compliments. I consider myself to have been very clumsy in this case. I'll take another short libation if you don't mind."

Wilbur poured himself a small portion.

"And you see, murder will out," Wilbur went on. "Back in Chicago the Morleys dreamed that they were well on their way to wealth. It seemed that Morley's scheme was working to perfection. All that the Scotts owned was to be theirs, the money embezzled from the bank and the collected insurance money. With a fortune so garnered they intended to disappear abroad. Mrs. Morley was to simulate Mrs. Scott and ostensibly marry Morley. He was to use an assumed name. There's where more ingenious work was done. Mrs. Morley was done over by a beauty surgeon. And I must say the surgeon did a remarkable job. He made an exact double of Mrs. Scott out of Mrs. Morley except in one slight particular, a thing which might have escaped less keen observation than mine. There was a mole upon Mrs. Scott's neck which the surgeon either could not make or which he forgot. When you see Mrs. Morley you will not know her. I have a photograph of Mrs. Scott. You will be able to see how cleverly things are done by surgery."

"Yes, I've seen some of the clever results of surgery," Jack put in. "That job with the Murphy button was terribly clever. The fellow that did that ought to take a postgraduate course in a plumbing school and learn how to swipe a joint."

"How much were the Scotts worth?" inquired Alice.

"Seven hundred and fifty thousand," replied Wilbur.

"Whew! Morley wasn't expecting to make much of a haul, was he?" exclaimed Jack. "A million! By the Gods, I don't know but what I'd bump off a female for a million."

"Jack!" exclaimed his wife.

"Yes, Morley had a real clever idea but like all the rest of the clever crooks he missed some seemingly unimportant details. When I had him cornered he attempted two more murders. He tried to kill detective Clarke and me."

"Lyman!" Alice screamed.

"You don't tell!" said Jack.

"He most certainly did. He had a bead upon me when Clarke shot the gun out of his hand. Morley's gun went off, but the bullet went wild. The second shot from Clarke's gun toppled Morley. That just about finishes the tale of the Morleys."

"But you haven't explained the shoes yet—nor the glove," said Alice with a smile.

"That's very easy. I never did mention the fact to you because you seemed worried about them, but I found out about the shoes before I left Summitville. You forgot about them, but you left a pair of your own at the cobbler's for repair. After you insisted that all of your shoes were accounted for I hated to tell you that you were mistaken for fear that you would gather the impression that I thought you knew something about the murder. And you were a little fidgety after the deed affair."

"You're right, I was," replied Alice. "And I did leave a pair at the cobbler's. It was a pair of shoes I particularly liked. I'm sorry I forgot, Lyman, really I am."

"Never mind, it wouldn't have made any difference had you remembered. It might have made more complications, that's all. Anyhow Morley saw those shoes in the cobbler's shop. They had a tag on them with your name on the tag. His astute mind worked fast. In view of the fact that his wife must come to the cottage the night he intended to murder Mrs. Scott, he reasoned that her footprints might give the affair away. He did not know that she wore her shoes off the same as you do. He knew you lived next door. Why not have it appear that you made the footprints of his wife? Should his plan fail and the murder he discovered, the footprints would direct suspicion against you. The shoes were just one of his cunning details the same as the glove. He noted in the bank that you had one finger missing and in some manner examined your glove when you laid it down inadvertently. He had one made to duplicate it, the one that was dropped purposely at Bakers Landing. He was a damned methodical cuss in a way and a sticker for details."

"But the plates that identified Morley?"

"Simple! Those in Scott's mouth were removed and Morley's substituted. Morley secured some new ones pronto."

"Hum!" exclaimed Jack. "It's almost unbelievable. But tell me! What about the liquor racket?"

"Oh yes," replied Wilbur with a laugh. "That's a good one too. I'd almost forgotten. Morley, Webb Tully and Fallows owned a distillery. It's located in the casket factory. Federal men are already on the way to take that over. Morley's cottage was used as a cache early in the game. But when the affair grew to proportions, this practice was abandoned. It has been a big business the last few years. They have shipped the stuff directly from the casket factory in caskets. And here's the laugh—Pelletieres' were the distributing agents in Chicago. Scott was the Big Shot, controlling all of Chicago's North Side. Federal agents probably have the Pelletieres by now."

"Well, I'll be a dumb onion!" said Jack in consternation as he held up his half filled glass of liquor. "Then this stuff isn't bonded."

"No," laughed Wilbur. "It isn't bonded. It's the old racket—pretty bottles and fake labels."

"But it tastes like the old McCoy."

"Sure it does. That outfit went after the liquor business with the same attention to detail that Morley used in his mad search of a million. They aged their stuff. Let's have some."

And with true prohibition spirit they took another "snifter" of the stuff that has made the name of Volstead famous.

"That explains the dynamiting, the attempt on our lives, the blowing up of the cottage, the altered court house record and everything," Jack remarked after a gulp.

"Precisely," returned Wilbur. "Those fellows in Summitville were afraid that our interest in the Morley case would cause us to discover their little game. It was too precious to give up. They tried to put us out of the way. If they had not done that I wouldn't have been at all anxious to inform the Federal authorities, for all things considered, the Coon Hollow has been a godsend. Now, does that clear up everything?"

"No, sir."

"What else?"

"What became of Pierre LaVell and what was his connection?"

"I fancied you'd get around to that. Well, eight weeks ago, as you know, the supposed Mrs. Scott buried her brother."

"Oh, I see!" exclaimed Jack in horror. "Another murder."

"Yes. The supposed brother was Pierre LaVell. Tomorrow two graves will be opened in the Rose Lawn Cemetery. In one I expect to find a casket which is filled with sacks of sand. In the other I expect to find a casket containing the body of Pierre LaVell. You see, Morley didn't want to give LaVell his cut."

"Greedy devils, these Morleys."

"Yes, and they firmly believed the age old motto: 'Dead Men Tell No Tales.' "

"But one dead man did—William Scott."

"As I have said before, the most carefully laid plans of crooks miscarry."

"But how did Morley get a burial certificate for Pierre LaVell? Surely his death was investigated."

"A dumb doctor probably made a case of ptomaine poisoning out of an arsenic highball."

"Well, that was taking an awful chance. Suppose the doctor really knew?"

"This doctor undoubtedly knew his Morleys."

"Oh, I see. They'd have killed him too."

"And of course Morley did not have on a blue serge suit," laughed Wilbur. "I knew that for certain after examining the hospital record. You did not notice it, Jack, but the date of Scott's operation did not correspond to the date of Morley's disappearance."

RAMBLE HOUSE's

HARRY STEPHEN KEELER WEBWORK MYSTERIES

(RH) indicates the title is available ONLY in the RAMBLE HOUSE edition

The Ace of Spades Murder
The Affair of the Bottled Deuce (RH)
The Amazing Web
The Barking Clock
Behind That Mask
The Book with the Orange Leaves
The Bottle with the Green Wax Seal
The Box from Japan
The Case of the Canny Killer
The Case of the Crazy Corpse (RH)
The Case of the Flying Hands (RH)
The Case of the Ivory Arrow
The Case of the Jeweled Ragpicker
The Case of the Lavender Gripsack
The Case of the Mysterious Moll
The Case of the 16 Beans
The Case of the Transparent Nude (RH)
The Case of the Transposed Legs
The Case of the Two-Headed Idiot (RH)
The Case of the Two Strange Ladies
The Circus Stealers (RH)
Cleopatra's Tears
A Copy of Beowulf (RH)
The Crimson Cube (RH)
The Face of the Man From Saturn
Find the Clock
The Five Silver Buddhas
The 4th King
The Gallows Waits, My Lord! (RH)
The Green Jade Hand
Finger! Finger!
Hangman's Nights (RH)
I, Chameleon (RH)
I Killed Lincoln at 10:13! (RH)
The Iron Ring
The Man Who Changed His Skin (RH)
The Man with the Crimson Box
The Man with the Magic Eardrums
The Man with the Wooden Spectacles
The Marceau Case
The Matilda Hunter Murder

The Monocled Monster
The Murder of London Lew
The Murdered Mathematician
The Mysterious Card (RH)
The Mysterious Ivory Ball of Wong Shing
  Li (RH)
The Mystery of the Fiddling Cracksman
The Peacock Fan
The Photo of Lady X (RH)
The Portrait of Jirjohn Cobb
Report on Vanessa Hewstone (RH)
Riddle of the Travelling Skull
Riddle of the Wooden Parrakeet (RH)
The Scarlet Mummy (RH)
The Search for X-Y-Z
The Sharkskin Book
Sing Sing Nights
The Six From Nowhere (RH)
The Skull of the Waltzing Clown
The Spectacles of Mr. Cagliostro
Stand By—London Calling!
The Steeltown Strangler
The Stolen Gravestone (RH)
Strange Journey (RH)
The Strange Will
The Straw Hat Murders (RH)
The Street of 1000 Eyes (RH)
Thieves' Nights
Three Novellos (RH)
The Tiger Snake
The Trap (RH)
Vagabond Nights (Defrauded Yeggman)
Vagabond Nights 2 (10 Hours)
The Vanishing Gold Truck
The Voice of the Seven Sparrows
The Washington Square Enigma
When Thief Meets Thief
The White Circle (RH)
The Wonderful Scheme of Mr. Christo-
  pher Thorne
X. Jones—of Scotland Yard
Y. Cheung, Business Detective

Keeler Related Works

A To Izzard: A Harry Stephen Keeler Companion by Fender Tucker — Articles and stories about Harry, by Harry, and in his style. Included is a compleat bibliography.

Wild About Harry: Reviews of Keeler Novels — Edited by Richard Polt & Fender Tucker — 22 reviews of works by Harry Stephen Keeler from *Keeler News*. A perfect introduction to the author.

The Keeler Keyhole Collection: Annotated newsletter rants from Harry Stephen Keeler, edited by Francis M. Nevins. Over 400 pages of incredibly personal Keeleriana.

Fakealoo — Pastiches of the style of Harry Stephen Keeler by selected demented members of the HSK Society. Updated every year with the new winner.

Strands of the Web: Short Stories of Harry Stephen Keeler — 29 stories, just about all that Keeler wrote, are edited and introduced by Fred Cleaver.

RAMBLE HOUSE's LOON SANCTUARY

A Clear Path to Cross — Sharon Knowles short mystery stories by Ed Lynskey.

A Corpse Walks in Brooklyn and Other Stories — Volume 5 in the Day Keene in the Detective Pulps series.

A Jimmy Starr Omnibus — Three 40s novels by Jimmy Starr.

A Niche in Time and Other Stories — Classic SF by William F. Temple

A Roland Daniel Double: The Signal and The Return of Wu Fang — Classic thrillers from the 30s.

A Shot Rang Out — Three decades of reviews and articles by today's Anthony Boucher, Jon Breen. An essential book for any mystery lover's library.

A Smell of Smoke — A 1951 English countryside thriller by Miles Burton.

A Snark Selection — Lewis Carroll's *The Hunting of the Snark* with two Snarkian chapters by Harry Stephen Keeler — Illustrated by Gavin L. O'Keefe.

A Young Man's Heart — A forgotten early classic by Cornell Woolrich.

Alexander Laing Novels — *The Motives of Nicholas Holtz* and *Dr. Scarlett*, stories of medical mayhem and intrigue from the 30s.

An Angel in the Street — Modern hardboiled noir by Peter Genovese.

Automaton — Brilliant treatise on robotics: 1928-style! By H. Stafford Hatfield.

Away From the Here and Now — Clare Winger Harris stories, collected by Richard A. Lupoff

Beast or Man? — A 1930 novel of racism and horror by Sean M'Guire. Introduced by John Pelan.

Black Beadle — A 1939 thriller by E.C.R. Lorac.

Black Hogan Strikes Again — Australia's Peter Renwick pens a tale of the 30s outback.

Black River Falls — Suspense from the master, Ed Gorman.

Blondy's Boy Friend — A snappy 1930 story by Philip Wylie, writing as Leatrice Homesley.

Blood in a Snap — The *Finnegan's Wake* of the 21st century, by Jim Weiler.

Blood Moon — The first of the Robert Payne series by Ed Gorman.

Bogart '48 — Hollywood action with Bogie by John Stanley and Kenn Davis

Calling Lou Largo! — Two Lou Largo novels by William Ard.

Cornucopia of Crime — Francis M. Nevins assembled this huge collection of his writings about crime literature and the people who write it. Essential for any serious mystery library.

Corpse Without Flesh — Strange novel of forensics by George Bruce

Crimson Clown Novels — By Johnston McCulley, author of the Zorro novels, *The Crimson Clown* and *The Crimson Clown Again.*

Dago Red — 22 tales of dark suspense by Bill Pronzini.

Dark Sanctuary — Weird Menace story by H. B. Gregory

David Hume Novels — *Corpses Never Argue, Cemetery First Stop, Make Way for the Mourners, Eternity Here I Come.* 1930s British hardboiled fiction with an attitude.

Dead Man Talks Too Much — Hollywood boozer by Weed Dickenson.

Death Leaves No Card — One of the most unusual murdered-in-the-tub mysteries you'll ever read. By Miles Burton.

Death March of the Dancing Dolls and Other Stories — Volume Three in the Day Keene in the Detective Pulps series. Introduced by Bill Crider.

Deep Space and other Stories — A collection of SF gems by Richard A. Lupoff.

Detective Duff Unravels It — Episodic mysteries by Harvey O'Higgins.

Diabolic Candelabra — Classic 30s mystery by E.R. Punshon

Dictator's Way — Another D.S. Bobby Owen mystery from E.R. Punshon

Dime Novels: Ramble House's 10-Cent Books — *Knife in the Dark* by Robert Leslie Bellem, *Hot Lead* and *Song of Death* by Ed Earl Repp, *A Hashish House in New York* by H.H. Kane, and five more.

Doctor Arnoldi — Tiffany Thayer's story of the death of death.

Don Diablo: Book of a Lost Film — Two-volume treatment of a western by Paul Landres, with diagrams. Intro by Francis M. Nevins.

Dope and Swastikas — Two strange novels from 1922 by Edmund Snell

Dope Tales #1 — Two dope-riddled classics; *Dope Runners* by Gerald Grantham and *Death Takes the Joystick* by Phillip Condé.

Dope Tales #2 — Two more narco-classics; *The Invisible Hand* by Rex Dark and *The Smokers of Hashish* by Norman Berrow.

Dope Tales #3 — Two enchanting novels of opium by the master, Sax Rohmer. *Dope* and *The Yellow Claw*.

Double Hot — Two 60s softcore sex novels by Morris Hershman.

Double Sex — Yet two more panting thrillers from Morris Hershman.

Dr. Odin — Douglas Newton's 1933 racial potboiler comes back to life.

Evangelical Cockroach — Jack Woodford writes about writing.

Evidence in Blue — 1938 mystery by E. Charles Vivian.

Fatal Accident — Murder by automobile, a 1936 mystery by Cecil M. Wills.

Fighting Mad — Todd Robbins' 1922 novel about boxing and life

Finger-prints Never Lie — A 1939 classic detective novel by John G. Brandon.

Freaks and Fantasies — Eerie tales by Tod Robbins, collaborator of Tod Browning on the film FREAKS.

Gadsby — A lipogram (a novel without the letter E). Ernest Vincent Wright's last work, published in 1939 right before his death.

Gelett Burgess Novels — *The Master of Mysteries, The White Cat, Two O'Clock Courage, Ladies in Boxes, Find the Woman, The Heart Line, The Picaroons* and *Lady Mechante*. Recently added is A Gelett Burgess Sampler, edited by Alfred Jan. All are introduced by Richard A. Lupoff.

Geronimo — S. M. Barrett's 1905 autobiography of a noble American.

Hake Talbot Novels — *Rim of the Pit, The Hangman's Handyman*. Classic locked room mysteries, with mapback covers by Gavin O'Keefe.

Hands Out of Hell and Other Stories — John H. Knox's eerie hallucinations

Hell is a City — William Ard's masterpiece.

Hollywood Dreams — A novel of Tinsel Town and the Depression by Richard O'Brien.

Hostesses in Hell and Other Stories — Russell Gray's most graphic stories

House of the Restless Dead — Strange and ominous tales by Hugh B. Cave.

I Stole $16,000,000 — A true story by cracksman Herbert E. Wilson.

Inclination to Murder — 1966 thriller by New Zealand's Harriet Hunter.

Invaders from the Dark — Classic werewolf tale from Greye La Spina.

J. Poindexter, Colored — Classic satirical black novel by Irvin S. Cobb.

Jack Mann Novels — Strange murder in the English countryside. *Gees' First Case, Nightmare Farm, Grey Shapes, The Ninth Life, The Glass Too Many, Her Ways Are Death, The Kleinert Case* and *Maker of Shadows*.

Jake Hardy — A lusty western tale from Wesley Tallant.

Jim Harmon Double Novels — *Vixen Hollow/Celluloid Scandal, The Man Who Made Maniacs/Silent Siren, Ape Rape/Wanton Witch, Sex Burns Like Fire/Twist Session, Sudden Lust/Passion Strip, Sin Unlimited/Harlot Master, Twilight Girls/Sex Institution*. Written in the early 60s and never reprinted until now.

Joel Townsley Rogers Novels and Short Stories — By the author of *The Red Right Hand: Once In a Red Moon, Lady With the Dice, The Stopped Clock, Never Leave My Bed*. Also two short story collections: *Night of Horror* and *Killing Time*.

John Carstairs, Space Detective — Arboreal Sci-fi by Frank Belknap Long

Joseph Shallit Novels — *The Case of the Billion Dollar Body, Lady Don't Die on My Doorstep, Kiss the Killer, Yell Bloody Murder, Take Your Last Look*. One of America's best 50's authors and a favorite of author Bill Pronzini.

Keller Memento — 45 short stories of the amazing and weird by Dr. David Keller.

Killer's Caress — Cary Moran's 1936 hardboiled thriller.

Lady of the Yellow Death and Other Stories — More stories by Wyatt Blassingame.

League of the Grateful Dead and Other Stories — Volume One in the Day Keene in the Detective Pulps series.

Library of Death — Ghastly tale by Ronald S. L. Harding, introduced by John Pelan

Malcolm Jameson Novels and Short Stories — *Astonishing! Astounding!, Tarnished Bomb, The Alien Envoy and Other Stories* and *The Chariots of San Fernando and Other Stories*. All introduced and edited by John Pelan or Richard A. Lupoff.

Man Out of Hell and Other Stories — Volume II of the John H. Knox weird pulps collection.

Marblehead: A Novel of H.P. Lovecraft — A long-lost masterpiece from Richard A. Lupoff. This is the "director's cut", the long version that has never been published before.

Dundee, Bill Pronzini, Gary Lovisi and James Reasoner.

Sand's War — More violent fiction from the typewriter of Ennis Willie

Satan's Den Exposed — True crime in Truth or Consequences New Mexico — Award-winning journalism by the *Desert Journal*.

Satans of Saturn — Novellas from the pulps by Otis Adelbert Kline and E. H. Price

Satan's Sin House and Other Stories — Horrific gore by Wayne Rogers

Secrets of a Teenage Superhero — Graphic lit by Jonathan Sweet

Sex Slave — Potboiler of lust in the days of Cleopatra by Dion Leclerq, 1966.

Sideslip — 1968 SF masterpiece by Ted White and Dave Van Arnam.

Slammer Days — Two full-length prison memoirs: *Men into Beasts* (1952) by George Sylvester Viereck and *Home Away From Home* (1962) by Jack Woodford.

Slippery Staircase — 1930s whodunit from E.C.R. Lorac

Sorcerer's Chessmen — John Pelan introduces this 1939 classic by Mark Hansom.

Star Griffin — Michael Kurland's 1987 masterpiece of SF drollery is back.

Stakeout on Millennium Drive — Award-winning Indianapolis Noir by Ian Woollen.

Strands of the Web: Short Stories of Harry Stephen Keeler — Edited and Introduced by Fred Cleaver.

Summer Camp for Corpses and Other Stories — Weird Menace tales from Arthur Leo Zagat; introduced by John Pelan.

Suzy — A collection of comic strips by Richard O'Brien and Bob Vojtko from 1970.

Tales of the Macabre and Ordinary — Modern twisted horror by Chris Mikul, author of the *Bizarrism* series.

Tales of Terror and Torment #1 — John Pelan selects and introduces this sampler of weird menace tales from the pulps.

Tenebrae — Ernest G. Henham's 1898 horror tale brought back.

The Amorous Intrigues & Adventures of Aaron Burr — by Anonymous. Hot historical action about the man who almost became Emperor of Mexico.

The Anthony Boucher Chronicles — edited by Francis M. Nevins. Book reviews by Anthony Boucher written for the *San Francisco Chronicle, 1942 – 1947.* Essential and fascinating reading by the best book reviewer there ever was.

The Barclay Catalogs — Two essential books about toy soldier collecting by Richard O'Brien

The Basil Wells Omnibus — A collection of Wells' stories by Richard A. Lupoff.

The Beautiful Dead and Other Stories — Dreadful tales from Donald Dale

The Best of 10-Story Book — edited by Chris Mikul, over 35 stories from the literary magazine Harry Stephen Keeler edited.

The Black Dark Murders — Vintage 50s college murder yarn by Milt Ozaki, writing as Robert O. Saber.

The Book of Time — The classic novel by H.G. Wells is joined by sequels by Wells himself and three stories by Richard A. Lupoff. Illustrated by Gavin L. O'Keefe.

The Case in the Clinic — One of E.C.R. Lorac's finest.

The Strange Case of the Antlered Man — A mystery of superstition by Edwy Searles Brooks.

The Case of the Bearded Bride — #4 in the Day Keene in the Detective Pulps series

The Case of the Little Green Men — Mack Reynolds wrote this love song to sci-fi fans back in 1951 and it's now back in print.

The Case of the Withered Hand — 1936 potboiler by John G. Brandon.

The Charlie Chaplin Murder Mystery — A 2004 tribute by noted film scholar, Wes D. Gehring.

The Chinese Jar Mystery — Murder in the manor by John Stephen Strange, 1934.

The Cloudbuilders and Other Stories — SF tales from Colin Kapp.

The Compleat Calhoon — All of Fender Tucker's works: Includes *Totah Six-Pack, Weed, Women and Song* and *Tales from the Tower,* plus a CD of all of his songs.

The Compleat Ova Hamlet — Parodies of SF authors by Richard A. Lupoff. This is a brand new edition with more stories and more illustrations by Trina Robbins.

The Contested Earth and Other SF Stories — A never-before published space opera and seven short stories by Jim Harmon.

The Crimson Query — A 1929 thriller from Arlton Eadie. A perfect way to get introduced.

The Curse of Cantire — Classic 1939 novel of a family curse by Walter S. Masterman.

novel of 70s Reno.

Writer 1 and 2 — A magnus opus from Richard A. Lupoff summing up his life as writer.

You'll Die Laughing — Bruce Elliott's 1945 novel of murder at a practical joker's English countryside manor.

RAMBLE HOUSE

Fender Tucker, Prop.   Gavin L. O'Keefe, Graphics
www.ramblehouse.com   fender@ramblehouse.com
228-826-1783   10329 Sheephead Drive, Vancleave MS 39565

www.ingramcontent.com/pod-product-compliance
Lightning Source LLC
Chambersburg PA
CBHW030335030726
47499CB00003B/777